The Pirates' Mixed-Up Voyage

DARK DOINGS IN THE THOUSAND ISLANDS

The Pirates' Mixed-Up Voyage

DARK DOINGS IN THE THOUSAND ISLANDS

Margaret Mahy

pictures by Margaret Chamberlain

Dial Books for Young Readers New York

First published in the United States 1993
by Dial Books for Young Readers
A Division of Penguin Books USA Inc.
375 Hudson Street
New York, New York 10014

Published in Great Britain by J. M. Dent & Sons Ltd.
Text copyright © 1983 by Margaret Mahy
Illustrations copyright © 1983 by J. M. Dent & Sons Ltd.
Design by Robert Olsson
Printed in the U.S.A.
3 5 7 9 10 8 6 4 2

Library of Congress Cataloging in Publication Data
Mahy, Margaret.
The pirates' mixed-up voyage / by Margaret Mahy ;
illustrated by Margaret Chamberlain.
p.   cm.
Summary: Captain Wafer and the crew of the Sinful Sausage
set sail for the Thousand Islands with a plot to kidnap a
famous inventor, only to be thwarted by a witch, a firedrake,
and the dastardly Dr. Silkweed.
ISBN 0-8037-1350-9
[1. Pirates—Fiction.]   I. Chamberlain, Margaret, ill.
II. Title.
PZ7.M2773Pm   1993   [Fic]—dc20   92-3931   CIP   AC

CONTENTS

The Pirates' Mixed-Up Voyage

DARK DOINGS IN THE THOUSAND ISLANDS

1   INTRODUCING LIONEL WAFER

There was once a young man called Lionel Wafer who was as hairy as he was handsome and as handsome as he was hairy. He was dissatisfied with living in real life, which was full of rules and regulations, and in his heart he dreamed of being a pirate.

This was hardly surprising, for he had been named after a pirate* (though not a very well-known one), and everything around him was somehow arranged to remind him of pirates. For one thing he was expected to dress as a pirate while at work, since he ran his retired uncle's tea shop, which was on the waterfront of the great city of Hookywalker. This particular tea shop was in a ship—a real ship—moored beside an old wharf, and it was called *Ye Olde Pyratte Shippe Tea Shoppe*. There were treasure chests and tropical islands painted all over the walls, and a big collection of ancient swords and fearsome firearms was displayed behind the counter. As well as all this, there was a parrot called Toothpick in a big cage in the middle of the tearoom—and, after all, there is nothing as piratical as a bright-green parrot, is there—especially when that parrot has a sign on its cage saying:

Please do not give rum to this bird.

*WAFER, Lionel—surgeon, buccaneer, and author. Believed to have been born about 1600. Gosse, Philip. *The Pirates' Who's Who.* Dulau and Co. 1924.

3

"Doom and destiny!" Toothpick would cry, for he was a determinist and believed that everything happening in the universe was part of a vast, mysterious plan. But Lionel Wafer believed in free will.

"What nonsense, Toothpick!" he would cry. "The world isn't run according to any plan, and that's that! In the heroic life things are simple, free, and unplanned."

2 Lionel Wafer Becomes Captain Wafer at Last

Curiously enough all the other people who worked in the tea shop wanted to become pirates too. For instance there was Toad, the cook—a man who seemed well suited for piracy because, although he didn't have a wooden leg, or a hook on the end of his arm, or anything quite as buccaneerish as that, he actually *did* have tin ears painted red.

"There's no real opening ashore for a man with tin ears," he would lament. "But at sea a man with tin ears is respected."

Tin ears or not, he was a man who would not hesitate to cook up pancakes, scones, or roly-poly pudding—and all by memory, for he couldn't read a word.

Then there was Brace-and-Bit, the waiter (a tall, thin, uncertain, nearsighted man, with a face to match), and Winkle, an extremely aged individual who swept up the crumbs after untidy tourists had eaten their scones and gone their way. Both these men declared they had yearned to be pirates from babyhood. They sang sea shanties beautifully, and they sang nautical songs that Brace-and-Bit had made up, but it seemed a pity that such rousing stuff should be wasted on landlubbers in a tea shop. Life seemed to be passing them by. If they could only be pirates, then everything would be different.

Evening after evening, when the tourists had gone home, Lionel Wafer would pull the gangplank up. Then

5

he and Winkle, Brace-and-Bit, and Toad would sit around one of the tea tables on the deck, under a sun umbrella, drinking a dangerous drink called rumfustion, out of teacups. They talked of burying treasure, or digging up treasure that somebody else had buried. Conversation dwelt on doubloons, ducats, and diamonds, on grog, ship's biscuits, and of course on walking the plank. They even imagined themselves finding the wonderful Noah's Ark Tapestry of the Hookywalker Museum, lost a hundred years earlier when a whirlwind* struck the city and blew down the museum and art gallery. A fabulous reward was being offered for the return of this masterpiece, but nobody sensible believed it would ever be found again.

It isn't surprising that, at last, all this dreaming became too much for everyone and, early one morning, Lionel Wafer himself cut the cable that bound *Ye Olde Pyratte*

*The whirlwind in question was the terrible Everlasting Whirlwind that roamed the Seven Seas of Romance and occasionally came ashore, spreading rack and ruin around it.

Shippe Tea Shoppe to the Hookywalker wharf, while, with his other hand, he broke a bottle of rumfustion over its bow and rechristened the craft with a wicked new name. From now on it was to be called *The Sinful Sausage*. Brace-and-Bit and Toad began pedaling, turning the old paddle wheels. Captain Wafer and Winkle hoisted the sails, and they set off for the Seven Seas of Romance, every man jack of them, along with Toothpick (but he was a parrot jack, of course).

What a fine, defiant sight they made leaving port, the deck bright with sun umbrellas and little tea tables (which, being bolted to the deck so that tourists would not steal them, had proved impossible to move, for none of the pirates had a wrench).

It was a big change for them all, but they were filled with courage, confidence, and good cheer... all, that is, except for gloomy Toothpick, who cried out from his perch on Captain Wafer's shoulder:

"Beware, beware! It's fate! It's fate!" And so on.

But of course no one paid any attention to the prophecies of a mere parrot.

BEWARE BEWARE

3   VERY REASONABLE AMBITIONS

The manners of pirates are usually very low, but they make up for this by having their hopes very high. Now that Lionel Wafer had actually become Captain Wafer, and Brace-and-Bit boatswain, Toad, of course, was made ship's cook, and old Winkle appointed cabin boy, a demanding job for a man with wobbly knees. They had left behind them real life with all its pettifogging rules and complications like library cards, dog licenses, parking meters, and phone bills, and they were all immensely hopeful.

Backward and forward over the bounding blue they sailed, keeping an eye open for the Everlasting Whirlwind. At first they did very well. They stole kippers from clippers, figs from brigs, lunches from launches, and so on, and what with these delicacies and some very hot and heavy gingerbread that Toad made, the first week went by quickly enough. However, though they had plenty to eat they did not seem to be getting very rich and, after all, a week seems a long time when you are yearning to make your fortune at once.

"Rumblebumpkin!" swore Captain Wafer—for now that he was a pirate he had become addicted to swearing. "We have been at sea a week, and so far all we have is a lot of figs and kippers and packed lunches. All very well in their way, but not to be compared with ducats, doubloons, and diamonds. It is not good enough. Look—I don't ask for much. I simply want to be a millionaire, that's all. Is that an unreasonable ambition?"

Everyone agreed it was not at all unreasonable. Brace-and-Bit, Toad, and old Winkle (and Toothpick the parrot too) agreed that all they wanted was to be rich as well, and swore that, if only life would grant them this simple wish, they would never ask for anything else ever again. They would retire at once and live simple lives in simple houses, with simple swimming pools and trampolines, becoming mellow and loved by all.

"It's no use saying that it can't be done," cried Captain Wafer. "Lots of people become millionaires. Think of Humbert Cash-Cash."

"He was an inventor though, wasn't he, Captain Wafer, sir?" asked Winkle. "Not a pirate." Brace-and-Bit looked doubtful too.

"He *is* a millionaire, Winkle," said Captain Wafer sternly, "and that is why I'm telling you to think of him."

4 THINKING OF HUMBERT CASH-CASH

All the pirates thought wistfully of Humbert Cash-Cash, for he was a man who had become enormously rich inventing useful things for people in the city of Hookywalker.

For instance, he had invented a useful rain drum for gardeners. You danced around, beating it, and after a few moments a light, refreshing rain fell on your greens. He had invented a very useful kind of peanut-butter sandwich, particularly good for school lunches, because every sandwich multiplied itself by four, provided you didn't open the lunch box and try to watch it happening. Then one of his best-known inventions was a particularly hot gingerbread designed especially for Eskimos and arctic explorers. One mere crumb made you glow like a potbellied stove. No wonder Humbert Cash-Cash had become a world-famous millionaire.

As the pirates thought about him, the parrot Toothpick squawked sarcastically, "Millionaire Cash-Cash—ha! He can read."

HE CAN READ

This hurt the pirates since none of them could read a word.

"Listen, you psittacotic critic," yelled Captain Wafer, "we're proud of not being able to read. We're pirates, not pedants!"

This forthright sentiment received general applause.

"Now listen here, mateys," cried Captain Wafer, "and you too, Toothpick," he added scornfully, "it's well known that Humbert Cash-Cash doesn't spend much time in Hookywalker these days. No! He's mostly off in his luxury sunshine retreat in the Thousand Islands* where he lives like a king in a house full of inventions, eating one peanutbutter sandwich after another, and never counting the cost, even though he can count better than most." (The pirates—who could not read—were not very good at counting, either.)

"True, Captain, true!" said Brace-and-Bit, his glasses sliding down his nose. "But how does that help us?"

"Well, I've just thought of a dastardly plan," said Captain Wafer proudly.

---

*The Thousand Islands mentioned here are not the Thousand Islands of the St. Lawrence River, but a totally different Thousand Islands never mentioned in geography books, so as to avoid confusion.

5 THE DIAMOND DOORKNOB PLAN

Captain Wafer paused and surveyed his crew; all eyes were upon him.

"Off we go to the Thousand Islands, and when we get there we land on the Cash-Cash Island, kidnap Humbert Cash-Cash himself, and purloin his inventions, or at the very least steal his doorknob. It is made out of a single great diamond, you know."

"That's a great idea, Captain," applauded Brace-and-Bit. "They say that that diamond doorknob is as big as a piano-mover's fist."

"Oh, it would be wonderful to have Humbert Cash-Cash himself on board," cried Toad. "My gingerbread would be sure to improve. He might teach me how to cook it—not the very hot gingerbread suitable for skiers, Eskimos, and people suffering from frostbite—but the sort we could all enjoy. Somehow I can't seem to get the hang of it."

"We aren't going to all this trouble to kidnap Humbert Cash-Cash just so that you can get the hang of cooking gingerbread, Toad," said Captain Wafer reprovingly. Meanwhile Brace-and-Bit began to look uncertain again.

"But Captain, how will we know which island belongs to Humbert Cash-Cash?" he asked. "I mean it's only one of a thousand islands, and a thousand is a pretty big number, isn't it? And they say there's all sorts living on those islands—witches, wizards, unicorns, even dragons they say. I mean, we wouldn't want to make a mistake in a region where dragons were commonplace."

"I don't want to meet a dragon, not with my knees," cried Winkle in anxious octogenarian tones.

"Avast there!" shouted Captain Wafer. "Stow that gab, Brace-and-Bit, or I'll stave you in like a rum puncheon. I don't choose to read or count, or any of that nonsense. But before we left I got the Hookywalker milkman (a lettered man who writes poetry and romantic novels when he isn't delivering the milk) to write the number of Humbert Cash-Cash's island down on a piece of paper. And that is

the same piece of paper I show you *now*...." Here the captain flourished a piece of paper with figures written on it. "All the islands in the Thousand Islands are numbered as if they were houses in a street, and all we've got to do is find the islands, sail in and out of them, and compare the numbers on the islands with the numbers on this piece of paper. We won't have to stop off anywhere, worrying wizards and witches by asking them the way to Island Six Hundred and Sixty-six (for such is the number in question). All we have to do is use our keen, piratical eyes and we'll be home and hosed, lads, home and hosed."

"Glory! Glory!" chanted old Winkle. "We'll be rich, rich!"

"That's about it, mateys!" Captain Wafer agreed, slapping his aged cabin boy on the back and sending him spinning across the deck. "Now, all we've got to do is to find the Thousand Islands. Mind you—that won't be easy."

But at that very moment a strange thing happened. It was one of those dull days you get from time to time, even in the Seven Seas; the Seven Seas were all gray and grumbling around the prow of *The Sinful Sausage,* yet suddenly the sun struggled through the clouds and painted the far horizon with gold. There, clearly revealed, lay the Thousand Islands, just over the edge of the world.

"There—you see!" cried Captain Wafer, boldly pointing to the horizon. "Look there!"

"Where?" asked Brace-and-Bit anxiously, looking in quite the wrong direction. His keen piratical sight was a little less keen than it should have been because his glasses had slid too far down his nose. But Toad saw the islands and was delighted.

"Wonderful," he cried. "Fortune flavors the bold!"*

"So it does!" Captain Wafer nodded. "Off we go! Pedal, men, pedal!"**

---

*An old cooking proverb.

**A command unique in the annals of piracy and recorded on page 10,002 of *The Guinness Book of Piratical Records.*

Only Toothpick stared sourly at the faraway lands, sus-picious of their green beauty. "Rumblebumpkin!" he swore. "Fate again! Oh well—I'll get a bit of sleep while I can."

RUMBLEBUMPKIN

6 THE UNEXPECTEDNESS OF ISLAND SIX HUNDRED AND SIXTY-SIX

Meanwhile the pirates began splicing the main brace, hoisting the topgallant, and pedaling away so that the paddlewheels went round and round. It was hard work, but they performed these nautical duties with hope and high spirits.

"They say that Humbert Cash-Cash has his house guarded by wolves and baboons," cried Captain Wafer, "but I put it to you boys—are we the ones to be worried by wolves or bothered by baboons?"

His confident crew laughed lightly at the thought of wolves and baboons, while *The Sinful Sausage* fairly skipped through the sea spray, until they arrived at last in the magical realm of the Thousand Islands. A soft breeze, scented with honey and cinnamon, wafted them on their way. The pirates saw hillsides of flowers that rose up fluttering in the air as the ship passed, and that turned out to be butterflies after all. They saw forests of blossoming trees darting with hummingbirds. Strange blue seaweeds washed out from the rocks as the sea breathed, and in and out of it played little schools of gold and silver fish.

"Really, Captain," said Winkle, tottering to the side and peering over with great interest. "Looking at them little fishes you'd swear Humbert Cash-Cash hisself had been emptying his money box into the sea."

"No poetry from cabin boys!" said Captain Wafer sternly,

but he couldn't help being moved by the old man's imagination.

Nor was this the only wonder of the seas that surrounded the Thousand Islands, for the ship was followed by several warble trout as it went on its way. These beautiful pink fish blew bubbles as they swam; the bubbles danced up to the surface of the water, and then on into the air. When they burst they gave off the scent of roses, lavender, and hot buttered toast as well as notes of lovely music, fragments of string quartets or of flute obbligatos.

Brace-and-Bit said that warble trout were well known for bringing good luck to a ship, and so, naturally, high spirits continued to be the order of the day.

The captain stood at the wheel, holding his bit of paper in his hand, watching out for Island Six Hundred and Sixty-six. This was not as difficult as you might suppose, for just as all the houses on a street have mailboxes with numbers on them, every island of the Thousand Islands had a big balloon floating above it, tied to a tree with ropes of scarlet or blue. Some of the balloons were quite plain—just purple or green or yellow—with no decorations at all, but others had wonderful patterns on them: pictures of ice

17

cream cones, birds, castles, lions, apples, dancing frogs, and galloping horses. However, one and all had the number of the island on them in black or red or gold, so, as *The Sinful Sausage* sailed along, the captain was able to study these balloons intently and to compare their numbers with the number written on the paper in his hand.

"That's the best one," he said, pointing to a particularly wonderful balloon. "I thought at first it was the sun, it's so golden and glittering, but the sun's over there and you don't get two suns in the sky at once—even in the Thousand Islands."

"Besides," said Brace-and-Bit, "it's got a basket hanging from it. That is an independent balloon, Captain. It isn't attached to any of these here islands. It's set out on its own."

"Not on its own," said Toad. "A man with glasses mightn't perceive this, Brace-and-Bit, but there's a person in that balloon looking out at us through a telescope."

"Never mind that," cried Captain Wafer suddenly. "I've got something better to look at . . . Island Six Hundred and Sixty-six. There it is. We've found it almost at once."

The pirates stared at the island he was pointing to. There was a long silence.

"That ain't what I'd call a very good-humored balloon," said Winkle doubtfully, looking up at the black balloon and at the sulky red figures that smoldered on its surface. "I thought balloons were meant to be joyous and exulta-

18

tious. I've seen sharks with more sunshine to them than that balloon up there."

"Likewise, the look of the island don't do nothing to raise a man's spirits," agreed Brace-and-Bit, staring at the beach that was covered in black sand and bones, and smelled of decaying fish. "This ain't my idea of the sort of island a millionaire would seek out for a tropical, sunshine retreat."

The island consisted of a pointed hill almost entirely covered with dark, depressing fir trees. A stormy cloud hovered over it, and as they watched apprehensively, there was a flash of lightning and the cloud growled at them like an angry dog. Everywhere else the sky was blue, and the sun shone down as cheerfully as a body could wish, but certainly Island Six Hundred and Sixty-six had a very threatening look about it.

"Another thing, Captain," said Toad, "I don't see that that there house is nearly as big as what we were led to believe. It's not what I'd call a mansion, not by no means."

The house was clearly visible on the tip-top of the island. There was no swimming pool to be seen, and it was certainly a small house, though a very pretty one. From the deck of *The Sinful Sausage* it looked like an iced cake. Yet as the captain stared, gnawing his lip in doubt, something sparkled, something shone on the green front door.

"Bumblerumpkin!" swore the captain. "It's the diamond doorknob, lads. Lower the jolly boat. We're going ashore."

"It's fate," squawked Toothpick. "That's what it is—fate again!"

IT'S FATE

19

But no one took any notice of the parrot.

Lowering the jolly boat cheered up the pirates. Soon the diamond doorknob would be in their hands and they would be at least halfway to being millionaires themselves. They rowed with high hearts (and oars too, of course), and within a few minutes the keel of the jolly boat grated on the black shore of Island Six Hundred and Sixty-six.

7 WINKLE FINDS SOME BITS AND PIECES

Once they had landed on that dread shore and were actually standing on the sand among the whitening bones, they rapidly grew thoughtful again. It is hard to be really cheerful when surrounded by the smell of decaying fish.

A signpost shaped like a terrible, thin hand pointed up some stairs. The pirates looked at it doubtfully.

"What does it say?" quavered Winkle. "Remember, I don't see as clearly as some."

"How can we tell what it says?" replied Toad proudly. "You know we can't read or write. It's pointing up, isn't it—up all those steps and stairs, zigzagging up the hill? So that's where we go. Up and up!"

"Up, is it?" cried Winkle bitterly. "And just what do you suppose a man of my age, and with knees like mine, thinks of up!?"

But the other pirates were already climbing the hill and, in spite of his knees, Winkle did not want to be left behind.

"Oh horrakapotchkin!" he mumbled, and was just about to start after them, when something lying on the black sand caught his eye. "Now that's very strange!" he said to himself. "Fancy those lying as if they were so many shells. It seems a pity to leave them there—not that they're much good to a man, I don't suppose. But then you never know." And he picked up the whatever-they-were that had engaged his venerable interest and put them in his pocket. Then he hurried on after the other pirates as fast as his thin, wobbly legs would carry him.

8 MEETING MRS. MANGLE

On and on up the hill, zigging and zagging, went the pirate crew. There were no flowers, hummingbirds, or butterflies on this island. But there were a lot of spiders, which alarmed Toad very much indeed, for there was something about the scuttling legs of spiders that he found detestable.

"I'd rather have wolves and baboons than spiders. The mere sight of one of them athwart my bow gives me a turn I'm slow to recover from," he warned everyone. Then he clapped his hands over his tin ears in case the spiders should climb in and spin sticky, gray webs.

"You yellow-livered galleyganger!" hissed Captain Wafer. "Pipe down and climb harder!"

Toad looked indignant at being called a yellow-livered galleyganger but he did as he was told, and at last, breathing hard, they came out at the very tip-top of the island, with the house right in front of them. It looked even prettier than it had from below with its doorknob glittering.

"Quick!" hissed the captain. "There it is now. Let's at it, lads," and he seized the doorknob, which came off in his hands instantly. It was so easy that he was taken aback, for he had been looking forward to a bit of a struggle. Meanwhile the other pirates had been gazing at the house in amazement.

"By the powers, Captain, there's something mighty odd about this place, and that's a fact," said Brace-and-Bit. "I've never beheld a diamond like that one before, in all my born days." He touched it and then licked his fingers. "It ain't even a diamond! That's a—why, that's a great, big lemon drop, that's what that is."

There was a soft, crunching sound. Toothpick the parrot was perched on the roof eating the gutter with great enthusiasm.

"Chocolate!" he squawked. "It's Lollipop Castle, shipmates."

"Gingerbread!" exclaimed Toad, examining the wall of the cottage. "Blow me down, it's gingerbread—very good gingerbread too," he added in a rather jealous voice. "These millionaires don't care, do they? They can afford anything. What luxury! The sugar and butter alone would cost a fortune."

But as the captain was standing, staring in horror at the great lemon drop in his hand, and Toad was exclaiming over the good quality gingerbread in the wall of the house, a voice from inside was heard saying,

Nibble, nibble mousekin
Who's nibbling at my housekin?

And slowly the peppermint-candy door creaked open. Out came a stoutish, motherly looking person in fluffy slippers

24

and a flowery apron. However, you can always tell a witch when you see one—there's something funny about their eyes. The pirates knew at once that they were looking at a well-established witch. She was wearing a hand-knitted cardigan and a tweed skirt, just as if she were an aunt. But there was absolutely no doubt about it, if only because she was wearing a couple of witch medals pinned to her cardigan—the Order of the Black Cat—and, most ominous of all, the great Warlock Whizzbang—a medal only given for the most advanced wickedness. They had walked straight into a witch's house, pulled her doorknob off, and allowed their parrot to eat her gutter. Just for a moment they wished they were safely back in real life.

9 THE TREASURE MAP

"Oh, dearie me," said the old woman, as if taken aback. "What a lot of visitors." She looked up at their parrot, and over at their swords. "Are you all pirates then, come to threaten poor old Ivy Mangle?"

"Oh, goodness, no!" exclaimed the pirate captain, thinking very quickly. "Dear me, no—not at all," he added, while his crew stood, looking guilty and terrified, with their swords in their hands. (Toothpick went on eating the gutter.) "We're—we're simply promoters of a wonderful set of encyclopedias, Mrs. Mangle. M'm, we're encyclopedia salesmen."

At these words a very curious look crept over Mrs. Mangle's face. Her nose twitched—an astonishing sight, for her nose was a particularly large one—and she bared her teeth. They were bright blue.

"We thought Mr. Humbert Cash-Cash might like to buy a couple of sets," mumbled the captain. "It's very scholarly."

"Well, perhaps he would," replied Mrs. Mangle, smiling broadly with her bright-blue teeth. "But I can't speak for him you know. He lived—that is to say he still lives—on Island Six Hundred and Sixty-six, you know."

"But this *is* Island Six Hundred and Sixty-six!" cried the captain, passing the lemon-drop doorknob to Brace-and-Bit, and sneaking a quick look at his bit of paper, which he had folded in his pocket. "I've got the number here."

The witch shuffled a few steps forward and looked at what was written there. Then she gave the captain a long look from her witchy eyes.

"You're holding it upside down, dear," she said. "Er . . . can't you read?"

The pirate captain hated to admit to a witch that he couldn't read.

"I can read as well as the next man," he said airily, but the next man was Brace-and-Bit, and he couldn't read either. The witch looked as if she suspected this.

"Are you sure you're encyclopedia salesmen?" she asked. "Where's your encyclopedia, then?"

"It's very heavy," the captain said cunningly. "We've left it down in the ship—that's what we've done. It's all in very big boxes . . . er . . . blue packing cases, actually."

At these words not only the witch's little red eyes but her blue teeth as well flashed dangerously. "I should like to see it," she said.

"Brace-and-Bit can tell you about it," gasped the pirate

captain. "He's—he's the expert." This was not very fair, but the captain was running out of ideas, and besides he knew Brace-and-Bit had a very peculiar talent. When terrified he would talk in rhyme—a habit that often confused the person he was talking to.

"It's a fish encyclopedia," cried Brace-and-Bit, inventing desperately.

"It's—well—it's incomparably useful for those that have dealings with fish," and he began to sing, just as the captain had hoped he would.

> Would you whisper to a whiting
> That the barracuda's biting?
> Would you help a flounder found a school of
>   fish?
> Would you caper with a kipper?
> Help a napper hunt the slipper?
> Then our book will be exactly what you wish.
>
> Would you share a mashed banana
> With a lonely old piranha?
> Would you let a lobster give a crab a kiss?
> If you ever feel you need a
> Good marine encyclopedia
> Then you couldn't get one fishier than this.

The witch opened her mouth to say something in reply to this fine song, but at that moment Toad, who had been quietly inspecting the gingerbread wall of the house, interrupted her.

"What gingerbread!" he exclaimed. "I've never seen anything like it. I don't suppose, Mrs. Mangle that, between cooks (for when I'm not selling encyclopedias I'm a great one for cooking) you'll let me have the recipe."

Of course this was mere flattery for, even if he'd had the recipe, Toad could not have read it. The witch smiled so widely it looked as if her face might fall in half.

"I'll get it," she said. "Don't go." And she vanished behind her peppermint door into her gingerbread house.

"Gingerbread!" the captain exclaimed between clenched teeth. "I'll give you gingerbread. What did you ask her that for?"

"Let's run," said Brace-and-Bit.

"Run!" quavered Winkle, who had been leaning against a fir tree trying to get his breath back after the long climb up the hill. "Are you asking a cabin boy who has passed his eightieth year and has just climbed up a thousand and six steps, and been horrificated by a witch with blue teeth—are you asking such a cabin boy to run for his life?"

"We could be halfway down the hill by now," Brace-and-Bit cried. "Come on, lads." But Mrs. Mangle popped out of her house again with an old, yellow paper in her hand.

"Here it is," she said to Toad. "It's a very old recipe—very old. You can have it, dear, for I know it by heart. I'm always having to cook up a batch for house maintenance, you know. I'm sorry," she went on in a very sly voice, "that this recipe is a bit of a mess, but there's a lot of stuff scribbled on the back, you see, dear. An old treasure map or something."

Toothpick the parrot let out a terrible squawk, and all the pirates stared at Ivy Mangle as if they couldn't believe what they were being told.

"It looks a very good recipe," said Toad slowly, taking it and holding it sideways. "Very toothsome!" He screwed his right ear in more securely. "Er—pardon me, Mrs. Mangle—you see I've got this little problem with my auriculars—but did you say there was a treasure map on the back of this recipe?"

"Yes—it's a map of Island Eight Hundred and Eighty-eight," Mrs. Mangle said. "There's a fabulous fortune buried on it somewhere."

"A fabulous fortune buried on Island Eight Hundred and Eighty-eight!" exclaimed Captain Wafer, making sure that the number was on the map. He nudged Brace-and-Bit, who nudged Toad, who nudged Winkle—who fell over.

"It's a wonderful opportunity for someone, but I expect you encyclopedia salesmen are too busy to bother about things like fabulous fortunes." Mrs. Mangle gave her blue, malicious smile. "Yours must be a full life. I suppose you won't have time to come in for a cup of tea and a lump of chocolate-berry scroggin?"

"That's very true, Mrs. Mangle, ma'am," exclaimed the captain. "But it's our job to trace Humbert Cash-Cash, so, begging your pardon, we'll be on our way with many thanks for this fine treasure map—that is to say, this notable recipe for gingerbread that we all love, man and boy."

"Would you like your doorknob back, Mrs. Mangle, ma'am?" asked Brace-and-Bit, offering her the great lemon drop that he had been holding all this while. But she shook her head.

"I'll boil up another," she said. "They're never the same once they've come off like that."

So, with many nervous salutations and falsely amiable smiles, the pirates began to scramble back down the long flight of steps. The captain held the map, which he had firmly taken from Toad. Brace-and-Bit carried the lemon drop, and Toothpick sat on Winkle's shoulder, laughing sarcastically whenever the ancient cabin boy stumbled a bit.

Mrs. Mangle listened to them going with a knowing smile on her face. She shuffled her feet in their woolly slippers, and looked out over the sea to one particular island of the Thousand Islands, plain to see from her high hilltop perch.

Then she kissed her hand to the island in a very wicked way.

"There you are, my dear," she murmured. "Don't say I don't do anything for you. A delicious meal is coming your way. Oh Mangle, Mangle, how I miss you, but women sometimes have to decide between love and career."

From her apron pocket she took out a little lemon drop, which she clapped onto the spike sticking out from her door—all that was left of a once-proud doorknob. She muttered a few words and made a magical gesture. The lemon drop began to grow and shine with a sort of yellowish white light. From a distance it did look rather like a diamond.

10   A LOST MEMORY

Of course by now the pirates had totally forgotten about kidnapping Humbert Cash-Cash, and intended to go to Island Eight Hundred and Eighty-eight and dig for treasure immediately. They did not realize how very tricky and treacherous witches can be. There was a spanking breeze, so none of them had to pedal, and all seemed set for the uninterrupted discovery of enormous wealth. But then something happened that took their attention away from the treasure for as much as twenty minutes.

Brace-and-Bit had just polished his glasses and noted through them something blue bobbing about over the waves. He pointed this out to the captain.

"Flotsam or jetsam," declared Captain Wafer. "It's one or the other, but I can't tell which. However, shiver my deadlights, we'll have it on deck and see what it's all about. It looks like a packing case, but who ever heard of a blue packing case floating around on its own?"

"It's getting closer," cried Toad in an excited voice. "It looks very shipshape, Captain, as if it might contain something worthwhile. Suppose, just by chance, it was the lost Noah's Ark Tapestry of the Hookywalker Museum."

"And there," said Brace-and-Bit, gazing upward, "is that golden balloon again." He sounded puzzled. "Anyone would think it was following us around, watching us through a telescope."

"Never mind that!" snapped Captain Wafer. "Heave and haul, Brace-and-Bit. Let's get this packing case onto the deck. Don't let yourself be distracted from the main business of piracy by golden balloons."

They hauled the packing case onto the deck, with many a "Yo heave ho!" and so on, but when they opened it there wasn't a single bit of treasure in sight. What a disappointment! The packing case held nothing but a small, mousecolored man in red pajamas, fast asleep and carefully packed in a lot of pink-and-white tissue paper.

"Someone has packed him very carefully," remarked Brace-and-Bit, trying to look on the bright side of things. "He must be worth something to somebody."

"He's waking up!" whispered Toad. "Let's hear what he's got to say for himself."

The sleeper mumbled and wrinkled his nose, then he opened round, blue eyes, winked, blinked, rubbed his eyes, and winked again. But no matter what he did he could see nothing but pirates looking down at him.

"Who are you?" he asked in an astonished voice, a question that seemed fair enough under the circumstances.

"Tell us who you are first," said Captain Wafer. "We're pirates, we are, and we've just pulled you out of the sea. We thought you might be something of value."

The man blinked some more. He sat up and began feeling his arms and legs in a bewildered fashion.

"You're quite right," he said at last. "I am of value. I'm convinced of that—but—but—who am I?"

This did not seem a reasonable question to ask pirates who had only just met him.

"Don't you know who you are?" cried Toad in lively astonishment.

"I haven't the faintest idea," he admitted. "I can't remember who I am, or where I am, or *why* I am. I do believe I've forgotten everything I ever knew."

"By the powers!" exclaimed Brace-and-Bit. "He looks as if he could be a seafaring man. He's tattooed in red and blue all over his chest."

It was true—they could see that, under the half-open red pajamas, the stranger's chest was covered in red-and-blue tattooing.

"That doesn't look like the tattoo of a seafaring man to me," remarked Toad, looking at it with deep suspicion. "That looks more like the tattoo of a librarian or a university lecturer."

The tattoo did not show anchors or mermaids, or anything that a natural man might wish to have inscribed on him. It was in several columns of red and blue print—small print too.

"It looks like poetry!" Captain Wafer cried. "But what

34

sort of a sentimental swab goes around getting himself tattooed in poetry. What does it say?"

The man looked down at his tattoo in a squinting fashion.

"Look—I don't know," he said, shaking his head. "I can't—I can't seem to remember anything at all. I've forgotten how to read."

"And you've got nothing in your noodle to help us find out what you are doing bobbing about in a packing case here, among the Thousand Islands?" exclaimed the captain incredulously. "Well, all I can say is—that's outside of enough!"

"It beats the band!" grumbled Brace-and-Bit. "His mind's an absolute blank. But wait a moment—do you have any clue in the pocket of your pajamas?"

The packing-case man immediately turned out his pajama pockets. There was nothing in them but a few pieces of jigsaw puzzle and a small photograph. He studied the photograph, frowning in a puzzled way.

"There's something written here," he said at last, "but, as I told you, I can't remember how to read. Perhaps you could read it for me."

"Do we look like the sort of freshwater swabs that go in for reading?" growled the captain, snatching the photograph. "Here, let me clap my deadlights on it and . . ."

But at that moment the captain's voice failed, and he blushed as red as a rose, struck to silence by what he saw. The photograph was of a female person of wonderful beauty, with soft brown eyes, and skin like rose petals. Funnily enough she was standing beside a hot-air balloon and wearing pink-and-white striped overalls, and an attractive pink crash helmet. She certainly presented a sharp contrast to Mrs. Mangle.

"What a little bobbydazzler!" exclaimed Brace-and-Bit, but though he spoke very respectfully, even this simple comment made Captain Wafer grind his teeth together in a jealous rage. It is easy for a handsome, hairy pirate, leading the simple, romantic life, to fall madly in love at a moment's notice, and this is what had happened to the captain. From that instant he was consumed with love for the beauty in the photograph.

Still, none of the other pirates had fallen madly in love. They were still thinking about treasure, and the captain knew they were depending on him. Though he longed to go on gazing at the photograph of the loveliest woman in the world, he pulled himself together with a mighty pull that shook him to his very bootlaces. Slipping the photograph under his vest (about where he thought his heart was*), he now began to consider what to do with the packing-case man.

Brace-and-Bit was all for making the new man walk the plank, but Toad, who was tenderhearted, merely wanted to maroon him, while Winkle whiffled away so indistinctly that it was hard to make out what he was voting for. How-

---

*Actually he placed it over his liver, owing to ignorance, but he *intended* to put it over his heart and that's what counts (except, of course, in major surgery).

ever, the man objected both to marooning and to walking the plank.

"I know I'm a man of value!" he said boldly. "I feel it *here,*" and he placed his hand on his heart with great sincerity. "Look at all that pink-and-white tissue paper! No one goes to that sort of trouble packing up a man who's worth nothing, and I'm sure you'd regret getting rid of me. Forget about making a man of value walk the plank! Why don't I come along with you and be a pirate too?"

Captain Wafer was about to object to this but Winkle came tottering forward, looking at the packing-case man with sharpened interest. He seemed particularly interested in his knees.

"Begging your pardon for speaking out, Captain," he said in his quavering way, "but how about this? You let me be coxswain from now on, and this flotsam and jetsam can be cabin boy in my place. He's got the knees for it, you see. You need good knees for cabin boy work and it's the one thing—the two things really—that I haven't got. Yes, he can be cabin boy and, as he hasn't got any name he can recall, we'll call him Packy, after the packing case he came in."

"That would suit me very well," Packy agreed rapidly. "I somehow feel I might have talents in the cabin boy direction."

So it was settled, and rather quickly too, for the pirates felt impatient to be done with all this flotsam and jetsam business and to be off after the golden treasure on Island Eight Hundred and Eighty-eight. Toad led Packy off to instruct him in his cabin boy duties.

"More doom!" squawked Toothpick from the captain's shoulder, just to remind them that fate still had its eye on them.

Only Winkle stayed for a moment, guided by who

knows what piratical instinct. He fumbled around in the pink-and-white tissue paper vaguely searching for something, and then an expression of satisfaction crossed his wrinkled countenance.

"Very good!" he mumbled. "Very good! Why, if I get any more of these I'll get the whole picture. I'll just go on keeping my eyes open, and who knows what I might end up with!"

And he put the things into his pocket and struggled off to set about his new nautical duties as coxswain.

11   Following a Treasure Map

Captain Wafer spread out the treasure map on a tea table. The moment they saw it the pirates knew they were in luck. There was the outline of a large, respectable-looking island, and in the middle of it, a big cross painted in red and gold.

Off went *The Sinful Sausage* in and out of the Thousand Islands. Down in the galley Toad was putting together a picnic basket. His best tin cookie cutter, shaped like a pirate, was at his elbow. He was teaching Packy how to make gingerbread and cut out gingerbread pirates. Packy was learning with great speed, though he showed an unfortunate tendency to try and put in ginger by the cupful.

"We pirates like our gingerbread hot," Toad said, "but not *that* hot." He took the cup away from Packy. "You'll have to watch your tendency to overginger."

"It *felt* right," Packy complained.

"Yes, it might feel right," said Toad, "until you tasted it, and then you'd see whether it felt right or not. Now get on and pack the rum into the picnic basket. It's not a proper pirate picnic without ample rum."

At last they came to Island Eight Hundred and Eighty-eight. Warble trout were swimming in the clear green water, and the waves lapped soothingly on a white beach covered with pink shells. A big, silver balloon was tied to a palm tree and, clear for all to see on its shining surface, were the numbers 888. How the pirates cheered!

"Now that's something like an island, that is," said Brace-and-Bit with approval. "You can tell there's good fortune waiting there, mateys."

"What will be, will," said Toothpick sourly. "Fate again!"

"Stow that gab!" said the captain sternly. "Of all the unaccountable birds, Toothpick, you're the worst."

Looking at that lovely island sparkling in the sun, harmonious with the music of warble-trout bubbles, you and I might have thought of swimming and sunbathing, but these pirates were mad for treasure. They launched their jolly boat, sprang on board—Toad clasping the picnic basket—and set off for the shore. When they arrived they leaped out onto the sand, and it was but a moment or two before Toad discovered a promising signpost in the shape of a pelican, carved out of solid marble. With its great pelican beak the signpost pointed down a wide and easy track among the breadfruit trees, but the two words on the signpost read:

WATCH OUT!

Not being able to read, the pirates did not take any notice and plunged along the track, shouting with triumph, as if the treasure were already in their hands.

After a while they came to another signpost, this time in the shape of a flamingo.

DANGER!

read the signpost and pointed in the very direction they were going in.

"Off we go, lads, there's a fortune waiting for us," shouted Captain Wafer. "Be bloody, bold, and resolute," he added, quoting Shakespeare—most unusual in a man who couldn't even read.

On they ran, Packy coming last, out of respect for the other pirates, and Winkle coming second to last, out of respect for his knees. Finally they reached a clearing and knew at once that their search was nearly at an end.

The clearing was set among beautiful groves of bread-fruit trees and wrangleberry bushes, covered with clusters of red and blue wrangleberries. In between the bushes the ground had a curious scorched look that would have made anyone less excited than Captain Wafer was think twice.

There, in the middle of the clearing, just as he had hoped, was a big trapdoor with a red-and-gold "X" painted on it.

The pirates walked all around the trapdoor, admiring it from every possible angle. No matter from which direction you looked, it promised adventure and fortune. So, without more ado, they began to hoist it open. With well-oiled ease it revealed a pit of cloudy darkness below. At first the pirates could not see a thing.

"I don't see any diamonds," grumbled Captain Wafer. "I'm sure they're there but—"

"I can see something glittering!" exclaimed Brace-and-Bit. "But just what it is—shiver my sides—I can't be sure. It seems to be moving." Then he gave a gasp and a cry.

The pirates leapt back as one pirate, for they had suddenly seen just what was rising out of the darkness underneath the trapdoor. And it wasn't a fabulous fortune. Out of the hole came the head of an enormous firedrake—a great serpent, more of a dragon really, breathing a little smoke as it looked hungrily at them. Eyes like smoldering coals glared from either side of a mouth full of long, sharp, red-hot teeth. Nostrils flared like crimson caverns. For a moment nobody said a word, and when at last somebody did, it was the firedrake.

12 ESCAPING FROM FIREDRAKES

"Oh, hello," it said in a pleased voice. "Another lot already. I suppose you annoyed my old weasel of a wife in some way. What she'd do without me, *I* don't know. The Thousand Islands would be seething with her enemies if I didn't eat them up for her."

"Eat us up?" whined Toad. "You wouldn't eat us up, would you?"

"I certainly would," the firedrake replied. "This island is Eight Eight Eight by number, and ate-ate-ate by nature. Everyone who comes here gets ate-ate-ate, you see." The firedrake threw back its head and laughed at its own joke, shooting a fountain of fire far up into the air. Then, seeing that the pirates were only smiling weakly, it stopped laughing and looked at them with a rather hurt expression (as far as they could make out).

"There's nothing personal in it, you know. The only person I really enjoy the thought of eating is my wife— and of course she doesn't come here very often. She knows I'm just waiting for my chance! Mind you, I nearly got her three days ago, but she was too quick for me."

"Your wife, by the powers! Your wife!" exclaimed the captain. He wasn't good enough at math to put two and two together, but he was starting to realize just what had happened. "Do you mean Mrs. Mangle is your wife?"

"She certainly is," said the firedrake. "I'm Mangle, you

know . . . not that you'd recognize me, of course. I wouldn't expect it. Wizard Mangle I was, in those far-off, halcyon days before I met you-know-who. Anyhow, I married her, and before I knew what she was about, there she was, helping me with my work, putting my books away after I'd finished with them, sweeping up after me, and so on. Learning all my secrets! I should have seen what was coming. One day it turned out she'd learned enough to change me into a firedrake. She was always a bright girl—too bright by half I'd say, with hindsight. However here I am, boring on. You didn't come here to listen to a lot of family gossip."

"No, we didn't. We came looking for treasure," the captain explained. "And of course we'll share the treasure with you now we know you're here."

"What treasure?" The firedrake looked suddenly alert.

"Making so bold, Mr. Firedrake, sir, there's a fabulous treasure buried on this island," Brace-and-Bit began. "We've got a map that shows where it's buried."

"Besides," said Winkle, "there was signposts, and if a man of my age can't rely on signposts, well, what can he rely on?"

"Let's have a look at this map," the firedrake said. "Come on, hurry up, or I'll scorch you a bit. What have we here?" He bent his head over the map, and then he swore in firedrake language.

"Gurgleschwitz! That's just a recipe for my wife's gingerbread. I know it well. There's a big demand for it from witches who are building new houses."

"Oh, the map's on the other side," began Toad eagerly.

"Save your breath," the firedrake said. "You can't trust anything with my wife's handwriting on it. Of all the treacherous traitors, she's the worst. As for the signposts—didn't you read them?"

45

There was silence from all the pirates.

"We just glanced at them," Captain Wafer said. "I thought I saw the words *doubloons and diamonds* on one of them."

The firedrake burst into a hideous yell of laughter that toasted the breadfruit on several nearby trees.

"You can't read!" he shouted. "You ignorant hoddy-doddies. No doubt about it, you deserve to be eaten! Oh well—that's evolution at work.... if you can't read you won't get by. It's a great natural proposition," he added. "It gives a sort of nobility to your end."

The pirates were not comforted by this.

"Well, now," said Captain Wafer, "it doesn't have to come down to a matter of actual eating does it? I mean— look at me, covered with hair. Look at Brace-and-Bit's glasses, and Toad's tin ears! Do we look appetizing? And what about Winkle, there? He's eighty-seven!"

"Eighty-nine," cried Winkle hastily.

"You wouldn't insult your stomach with Winkle, would you?" asked Captain Wafer incredulously. "Look—we'd disagree with you, no doubt about it."

"I didn't say I'd enjoy eating you," said the firedrake defensively. "I didn't say you looked tempting. But I never turn down anything she sends me, you know. I'm trying to *lull* her, and then when she's *lulled*, I'll *strike*. No sense in hurting her feelings until then, is there? Or yours, for that matter."

"Our feelings wouldn't be hurt," quavered Winkle. "We can get by without flattery, can't we boys?"

"Your feelings would be hurt—very hurt—deep down," the firedrake firmly contradicted him. "Mind you I don't say I wouldn't prefer gingerbread, because I would. Gingerbread washed down with a tot of rum would be a treat to me after the explorers, encyclopedia salesmen, and other

46

unappetizing trifles that she's sent me. She once sent me a man who'd called trying to sell insurance. Well I ate him all right, but he sold me some insurance first. I'm insured against damage by hail I am. So you see I'm not going to choke over a pirate or two."

"Did you say gingerbread?" asked Toad. "As it happens, I've got a picnic lunch with me, and in it is a batch of gingerbread pirates and a big flagon of rum."

"Have you?" exclaimed the firedrake, with deep interest. "Have you really? Is it really *hot* gingerbread? I like it very hot. It's not, by any faint chance, the Humbert Cash-Cash gingerbread, is it? Or even the Ivy Mangle gingerbread? Those explorers I mentioned had some Humbert Cash-Cash gingerbread in their South Pole emergency kit, and I've never forgotten it. I'd fly a hundred miles for some of the Humbert Cash-Cash commodity."

"It ain't either of those sorts," Toad said. "But it's a pirate gingerbread, and it's got so much ginger in it you'd swear you was devouring red-hot coals. Open that picnic box, Packy, and let him see what we've got there."

47

The firedrake was delighted with the contents of the pirates' picnic box.

"Now that's something I like," he said. "Gingerbread pirates and a flagon of rum." And so saying, he ate the gingerbread and drank the rum while the pirates watched rather wistfully. Not one of them but felt he could have done with a noggin of rum himself.

"I'll just wait for that to settle down," said the firedrake hiccuping a little. "Oh I *did* enjoy that. The gingerbread was not at all bad, not as hot as the Humbert Cash-Cash gingerbread for Eskimos and arctic explorers, but quite acceptable." He yawned a bit, and his eyes blinked dreamily.

A desperate plan crept into the pirate captain's mind.

"Would you mind if we sang a bit to keep our nerves steady?" he asked in a pitiful voice. "We want to die brave, see, and waiting comes hard to a man who's going to be eaten shortly."

"Oh, be my guests!" said the firedrake, mellowed by rum and gingerbread. "I like a nice tune. Of course if you sing badly I might have to eat you a bit sooner in self-defense."

"Lead us off, Brace-and-Bit," said the captain, nudging his boatswain in a meaningful way. "You say the words and we'll join in with the harmony. Something *drowsy*."

Brace-and-Bit looked blank for a moment and then gave a knowing wink, leading the pirates in a sort of lullaby. The pirates sang very mellifluously. With winks and nods they stood in line and harmonized beautifully with Brace-and-Bit.

> *Hushaby firedrake so hot to the touch,*
> *Eating explorers and pirates and such.*
> *Lie in a layabout, languorous laze,*
> *Dreaming of dallying, doze-around days.*

The pirates' voices rose in sweet harmony, and the fire-drake blinked and yawned. Actually the pirates yawned too, including Brace-and-Bit, though they were relying on him to make up the words. It was such a soporific song.

> *Lullaby firedrake so drowsy and dumb,*
> *Dreaming of gingerbread flavored with rum.*
> *Fritter and fool away, footle and flag,*
> *Slouch around, slack about, slumber and sag.*

The firedrake's snout sank down onto his claws and Toad saw, with somnolent astonishment, that his companions were looking dreadfully drowsy.

"This is no good," he muttered and quickly unscrewed his tin ears so that he couldn't hear the go-to-sleep song they were singing to the firedrake. Then he shoved Brace-and-Bit in the ribs so that he woke up and went on with the last verse.

> *Lie fallow firedrake and wallow unwitting,*
> *Oars are for resting on, hay is for hitting.*
> *Day dawdles droopily, beautifully boring,*
> *Firedrake sleeps soupily, sluggishly snoring.*

By the time the song was truly ended, not only the fire-drake, but every pirate except Toad was totally oblivious. Quickly Toad screwed his tin ears back in again and woke the other pirates as quietly as he could.

Off they ran, flat out through the wrangleberry bushes and the breadfruit trees, Winkle straggling behind (but not far behind), until they came out safely on the shore.

"What brilliance!" cried the pirate captain, slapping himself on the chest. "We actually sang a firedrake to sleep. This will go down in *The Pirates' Who's Who*—you may lay to that!"

Packy cleared his throat.

"That *will* be nice!" he said. "But what a pity we'll never be able to read it."

"Of course we'll be able to read it ..." began the captain, and then fell silent. The pirates looked at each other.

"Shiver me timbers, he's right!" exclaimed the captain at last. "Now, if I'd been a literary man I wouldn't have got that there number upside down, would I?"

"We would have been able to read the signposts," said Toad.

"And the treasure map!" added Brace-and-Bit guiltily. "We could have avoided trouble and embarrassment."

"We could read the tattooing on Packy's chest," Toad added. "I've always thought that a man could get by without the printed word, but it makes you think, by thunder."

Over among the straggle of wrangleberry bushes that

grew along the edge of the beach, just before the sand began, Winkle was picking something up, and then another something. The other pirates ignored him. Since he was now coxswain, he should have been looking after the jolly boat and getting them arranged in it.

"Read!" the captain pondered. "Shiver my sides, shipmates, how can we learn to read at our time of life? If there was one among us with the gift, well, he could instruct the rest of us, but since we're all equal in ignorance, what's to be done? We can't sit at school in a row with a lot of little babies, or our dignity as pirates is gone forever."

A spasm crossed the face of Toad. He had had an idea.

"Now listen here, shipmates," he began, half whispering, and glancing over his shoulder. "I don't want this to go no further, but casting my memory back a bit a certain name comes to mind. I recall hearing of a certain place in Hookywalker, Dr. Silkweed's Academy, where reading was taught—among other things—and it's them other things what call for caution. It's a place to enter warily. You know Crooked Kenneth? He graduated there, and it's said that's where the Bop-a-Cop gang learned their arts. The Department of Education denies it exists, but word gets round for all that. And if you don't get your lessons right, they say you're never heard of again. A school like this would shock our tea-shop tourists but..."

"But it sounds the very school for pirates!" exclaimed the captain.

"Now suppose," Toad went on, "we was to go back to Hookywalker and ask around the docks and the backroom betting dens and the rum shops. Quite likely we could find out the location of this academy and apply to enter it. I'll warrant we'd be a match for them."

"Toad, you've got more sense than I would have given you credit for," cried the captain, "and what I say is—this

Dr. Silkweed had better watch out for himself and his academy, for either he'll teach us to read or *he'll* be the one never to be seen again, and you may lay to that!"

The pirates looked at him with admiration, but Packy said, "Don't you think we'd better get to sea again? That firedrake could wake up and come after us at any moment."

"Truly spoke, Packy, truly spoke!" said Brace-and-Bit. "Come on, Winkle, you tottering old area of devastation. I call him that," he added to Packy, "out of pure affection."

Winkle came quavering up. "I'm finding them everywhere," he said in a puzzled voice.

"Shiver my sides, Winkle!" growled the captain. "Let's get ourselves out of here and back on board *The Sinful Sausage*. These are dangerous waters for an unlettered man."

But no one thought to ask Winkle just what he had been picking up on Island Eight Hundred and Eighty-eight—Firedrake Island.

13   DR. SILKWEED'S ACADEMY

Between a supermarket that specialized in selling burglar's tools, disguises, and such, and a seamy-looking business called "Rent-a-Librarian" on one of the darkest streets of the great city of Hookywalker, was a tall, squashed-looking, brick building—actually the thinnest brick building in the world. Over the door was a sign that read: *Dr. Silkweed's Academy—Literature and Languages (Alive and Dead)*. Here came the pirates, early one morning, shortly after their encounter with the firedrake. They looked at the door for a moment or two, then knocked, fairly politely for pirates. A peephole in the door opened and a red eye looked out at them.

"What do you lot want?" asked a muffled voice.

"Why, matey—we want to learn to read," said the pirate captain. "We want to learn quickly, and we don't want any lily-livered teacher who's going to go all fainthearted at the sight of our swords and copper-colored countenances."

"Are you sure you're not school inspectors?" asked the voice. "We can't be too careful who we let in, you know."

"Do we look like school inspectors?" howled Brace-and-Bit. "Open up before we break the door down. We're pirates thirsty for knowledge, that's what we are."

"They're getting very cunning, these school inspectors," grumbled the voice as the door opened slowly. "They pretend they've come to read the meter or sell encyclopedias.

'We've got one,' I say to them, and I don't open the door. It's my job to keep them out, you see."

A huge figure was revealed—a man so enormous that, for a moment, standing beside him, the pirate captain looked less like a bear and more like a bandicoot.

"Thomas Sump's my name," said this figure, putting out a hand as big as a coal scuttle.

"Not Thomas Sump the famous piano mover?" cried Toad in a voice of admiration.

"Well, I used to carry a few pianos around," this large man admitted, looking modestly at his feet. "But then I

had a very nasty experience with one particular piano that I don't care to recall. All I do now is to lift the school piano onto the stage or off the stage, as the case might be. Mainly I teach sewing, these days, at this very school."

"Does it say anything about sewing on the board outside?" asked Brace-and-Bit. "I . . . I didn't read it closely."

"We haven't painted it in yet!" Thomas Sump replied. "It's a new class—an extra. We teach languages (alive and dead), and cross-stitch, hemstitch, buttonholing, satin stitch, featherstitch . . ."

"Running stitch?" suggested Winkle.

"No need," replied Thomas Sump. "Anyone can get a stitch running."

"Wish I could," muttered Winkle.

"I only do it to be near the woman I love," Thomas Sump went on.

"Who is she?" asked the pirate captain in a manner at once sympathetic and suspicious. Thomas Sump, who was leading them down a long and dimly lit corridor, stopped and looked at him solemnly.

"Who is she?" he asked. "Why she's Mrs. Hatchett, the wonderful widow without whom this academy would be lost. She taught me that 'without whom,'" he added proudly. "Oh, she's the one to teach people grammar and how to punctuate, I can tell you. If they makes a mistake she punctuates them with the point of her sword, you see, and that learns them. The point of education, she calls it. She's a real lady of letters, with letters after her name!"

"She sounds the one for us, then," swaggered Brace-and-Bit.

"And we want to learn quick," added Toad. "We don't want to hang around onshore for years. We're men of the sea, we are."

Thomas Sump opened a door.

"In here," he said. "Assembly's in the hall!" He gave them each a sheet of paper. "There's the school song. The words is writ down—I beg your pardon, I should have said *wrote* down—for them that don't know it yet. Just sit down quietly at the back."

The pirates were now in a hall that seemed to be crowded with scallywags, scoundrels, and scapegraces of various sorts and sizes. They felt quite at home at once, though they noticed—with scorn—that there were some children present too.

Dr. Silkweed and his staff were at the other end of the hall, on a little stage.

"Sump!" called Dr. Silkweed in languid tones. He was a tall, boneless-looking man with a high, pale, intellectual forehead and dark glasses. "Sump, lift the piano onto this stage, will you? We're waiting to sing the school song so you'd better jump, Sump." Thomas Sump stumped down the little hall and lifted the piano onto the stage, though not without some puffing and blowing. Even the pirates, who had had very little to do with pianos, could see that this one was quite unusual. It was not so much grand as grandiose, with twice as many notes as the usual kind of piano, most of them black and white, but with a number of red ones too. Toad felt Packy give a start of surprise at the sight of it and turned to look at him curiously.

"Just for a moment the sight of that piano made me remember something . . . but the memory was gone before I really had a chance to catch hold of it," Packy whispered. "A room with a view of the sea came into it, and a child, and a jigsaw puzzle, and an explosion. But now I can't remember what it means. It's gone, like a dream."

The pianist struck the opening chords.

"*Should* it sound like that?" asked Packy, bewildered.

"I don't know," Toad admitted, "but if *I* sounded like

56

that I'd either go to the ship's doctor or the piano tuner—
that's what."

But before their eyes the mystery of the piano's strange
sound was being solved, for Thomas Sump jumped onto
the stage, peered into the piano and pulled out a little girl,
shouting and kicking. Thomas Sump was firm, however,
and carried her over to a group of other children, making
her sit down in her place among them.

The school song began. Though the pirates couldn't join
in, they listened closely and enjoyed the jolly romping tune.

At Silkweed's Academy, Master or Madam, he
Glows as he shows you the way.
Any language or lingo he'll teach you, by jingo,
Provided you're willing to pay.

Pass over your dollar, you'll soon be a scholar
And people who thought you were dumb,
Who thought you were past it, will be flabbergasted
At seeing how bright you've become.

Some groan that their grammar
*   is taught with a hammer,*

57

With bribery, buffets, and blows,
But there's nothing that makes you get over mistakes
you
Have made, like a punch on the nose.

Your teacher will say more when armed with a clay-
more
A snickersnee, saber, or mace;
If a crossbow is present your thoughts effervescent
Will rapidly drop into place.

Oh, Silkweed's the master—he makes them learn faster,
His method's impressive but tough.
Indeed at his college, they're thirsty for knowledge,
They cannot learn quickly enough.

When assembly was dismissed, Thomas Sump gathered the new recruits and took them to Dr. Silkweed's office. He knocked on the door, opened it, and announced the new students.

"Thank you, Sump," came the doctor's voice from inside the study. "Come in, my dear fellows. *Entrez!*"

14 A TERRIFYING PICTURE

The pirate captain had been thinking furiously standing outside the study door: I'm losing my dignity as a man and pirate, he had thought. I was the terror of the Seven Seas for a whole week and here I am hustled from pillar to post, all meek and milky, at the convenience of some sermonizing schoolmaster!

So, at Dr. Silkweed's words, he bounded through the door, Toothpick the parrot screaming on his shoulder. He swooped around the desk, caught Dr. Silkweed by the lapels of his jacket, and jerked him up into the air.

"Now look here, matey!" he hissed through clenched teeth. "We want to learn to read—my shipmates and me. We don't want none of your soft soup, see."

"Soft *soap*!" corrected Dr. Silkweed calmly, dangling in the air. "It's soft *soap*, my man. I don't want to hear you get it wrong again."

"I said 'soup' and I meant 'soup,'" declared the pirate captain, furious at the correction. "I like soup I do, and I don't fancy soap, so don't try and haze my thoughts with your bibliomaniac book learning. We just want reading, and maybe a touch of writing on the side. Now state your terms or I will slit you to the gizzard."

Dr. Silkweed, though dangling in the air, appeared neither dismayed nor even surprised. His dark glasses sat squarely on his long nose, and he smiled blandly at the captain.

"My dear sir," he said, "have no fears. Your determination and directness do you credit. I like to see it. We have just the place for you. I'll fill out your enrollment forms at once, just as soon as you put me down."

The pirate captain, glowing with pleasure, lowered Dr. Silkweed into his chair. He had enjoyed himself and thought that he was in charge of the situation. But at that very moment, as he shone with triumph, his eye fell on a handsome picture decorating the wall behind Dr. Silkweed's desk. His face grew pale and his mouth fell open foolishly. There was no mistaking those shrewd eyes, that flowery apron or those fluffy slippers, nor the gingerbread house in the background. The person in the picture was none other than Mrs. Mangle.

Dr. Silkweed's study was very edifying and academic in appearance. The picture of Mrs. Mangle was painted in oils and set off by a handsome, carved frame. Above this was a heavy object that looked rather like a set of bagpipes. Seeing the expression of horror on Captain Wafer's face, Dr. Silkweed turned quickly around and leapt to the conclusion that it was this heavy object that had alarmed the captain. He had no idea that the pirate captain had met the person in the portrait.

"There is no need to fear, my dear sir," said Dr. Silkweed silkily. "The object that startled you is, I must admit, a flamethrower. However, I rarely use it and then only under circumstances of extreme provocation. The mere sight of a simple firearm relaxes my pupils wonderfully. And, anyhow, it is ridiculous even to consider the mere possibility of any discord between us ... I already like you more than I can say. I—I really keep that flamethrower there for sentimental reasons. It was an early invention of Humbert Cash-Cash—when he was only ten years old you know—and we regard him as one of the greatest minds produced by the city of Hookywalker. He was a pupil of this very school in his childhood."

Toad groaned slightly at the name, for Humbert Cash-Cash seemed to be haunting them like a ghost—always seen in the distance but hard to come face-to-face with. Brace-and-Bit rolled his eyes around the study and looked with distaste at the bookshelves. The shelf nearest to him was filled with a massive new encyclopedia, bound in blue and gold.

"Encyclopedias!" he muttered. "Wherever we go these days, somehow it's encyclopedias and the men that sell them. There's more coincidences in this life than a man can cope with."

"I can't help wondering about that piano," whispered Packy to Toad.

"So you want to learn to read ..." Dr. Silkweed was saying. "A wise decision! You'll never regret it. Oh, what a world of delight is opening before you! The glories of literature, the power and the persuasion of poetry ..."

"Now then, stop that bibble-babble and let's get started," said Captain Wafer shortly and sharply. "We want it over quick, you understand. Tell us what you can do for us so that we can begin to get our bearings."

"I'll place you in Mrs. Hatchett's class. It's made up of three Stubborn Orphans from the Deadlock Orphanage. They're sent over here especially to have lessons with Mrs. Hatchett. My only fear is that you might find them too much for you."

"Are you suggesting that we might find a bunch of mewling orphans too much for us?" The captain bared his teeth alarmingly, caught the painted eye of Mrs. Mangle, and looked away quickly.

"No such thing!" said Dr. Silkweed soothingly. "Of course not, dear fellow. Now, please place your golden doubloons in this money box and sign this paper (which simply says that if you suffer physical injury, or even death, as a result of taking our program of reading instruction you, or your heirs, will not hold the academy responsible). I will then take you to your first class at once."

"How did you know I had golden doubloons?" asked the captain suspiciously.

Dr. Silkweed gave his gentle smile and touched a little box on his desk. "The Numismatical Analyst!" he said lightly. "It scans anyone who comes into the room, detects and assesses the money they have on them, and lists the coins in order of their value. It's a Humbert Cash-Cash invention."

As the captain signed, Winkle, who had been hiding behind all the others and staring at the ground rather than encountering, by accident, the eye of Mrs. Mangle's powerful portrait, saw a small object he recognized at once.

"Look at that!" he muttered to Packy, who was listening to all that went on with an air of gentlemanly interest. "I keep on finding them everywhere."

Dr. Silkweed, carefully signing the agreement, did not

see Winkle bend over and scoop up the little pieces that were lying on the heavily patterned, priceless Persian rug. Nor did he see him show them to Packy.

"That's interesting," said Packy. "I've got a few of those myself."

"I picks 'em up here, and I picks 'em up there," Winkle went on. "I'll get a full set one day, I shouldn't wonder."

Toothpick, from his point of vantage on the captain's shoulder, suddenly screamed sarcastically: "Tools of fate! We're pawns in the hands of destiny!"

"Stow that talk, Toothpick," shouted the captain. "Stow that determinism. All shipshape, Dr. Silkweed? Then take us to our class, for we're anxious to engage reading in hand-to-hand combat, shiver my sides."

TOOLS OF FATE

15   A Doctor of Literature

The moment the pirates clapped eyes on their fellow pupils they saw what the doctor meant. The Stubborn Orphans were really tough, and so lively and defiant that three children seemed quite a crowd. There was Annie who was short and square and dark, with bangs that fell into her eyes, and who managed to look like all corners, like a little brown brick. Then there was Wolfgang, a frowning, threatening boy as thin and sharp as a dagger. Last of all there was a little thumb-sucking girl—the very child who had been dragged out of the school piano—and she had a dusty, tangled appearance. Not only that, she carried a terrible gray rag, about the size of a bath towel, around with her, and this object was called "Towelly." When the pirates came into the room Towelly seemed to be taking up more than its fair share of space, spreading over the desk and dragging onto the floor. The little girl was nicknamed Caramello because nobody had ever managed to find out what her name really was. She seldom talked, and when she did, it was in a chattering language all her own.

"Now children," said Dr. Silkweed, "we have five new pupils signed on with us today. Five pirates! Won't that be fun for us all! I do want you to give them a warm welcome—but not too warm. Remember that these pirates are new at our school, and it will all be very strange to them to start with. So we'll have to be good little friends to them, won't we? No teasing, tricks or tripping them over, or flicking their legs with Towelly. Now I hear Mrs. Hatchett coming down the hall. Remember she is the widow of the late Sampson Hatchett, world wrestling champion (tossed out of the ring of life, alas!), and treat her with respect. Have a nice day."

"The old buzzard!" muttered Wolfgang. "All he does is collect the cash while Mrs. Hatchett and the others do all the work."

The door opened and Mrs. Hatchett came in. The pirates couldn't help gasping with surprise. She was totally different from anything they had been led to expect in a school teacher. Even if she had not been the widow of a wrestling champion they would have treated her most respectfully.

She wore terrifying black boots and a belt all studded with spikes. At one hip swung a brass chain and at the other a rather dashing saber. Over this ensemble she wore the gown and hood of a Doctor of Literature.

"Right," she said. "Take out Book Six of the Silkweed Granulated Readers and begin work."

The children sent up a howl of protest.

"Not Book Six, Mrs. Hatchett, please—not Book Six. That's all long words, little print, and no pictures." Mrs. Hatchett, without hesitation, pulled out a pistol, hidden in the folds of her Doctor of Literature gown, and fired it in the air. Looking up, Packy noticed that the ceiling above her desk was peppered with bullet holes.

"Silence!" she cried. "One single solitary word more and I will shoot your school lunches into smithereens. I have five new pupils and I want you children to be quiet and good for a quarter of an hour. Now, you pirates—don't slouch and slump. Sit up with nice straight backs, open your desks, and take out Book One of the Silkweed Gran-

ulated Readers. That is the book with the burglar on the cover."

Up leapt the pirate captain.

"No mere female woman, even if she is a Doctor of Literature, is going to tell me what's what," he declared fiercely. "Now if we want to have our backs straight, we'll straighten 'em, and if we want to have them crooked, we'll have 'em crooked, and you may lay to that!"

"Avast there!" said Mrs. Hatchett sternly. "You'll do as you're told like everyone else aboard this class. I am a teacher of the old-fashioned, bullying kind, and nothing's going to change that, least of all a weevil like yourself. You couldn't burrow your way into a ship's biscuit."

"Those who live will see," said the captain, drawing his sword.

"Indeed they will, you cormorant!" cried Mrs. Hatchett, drawing hers.

The orphans all seemed to be sitting calmly and straight-backed at their desks, barely paying any attention to the argument, but somehow someone managed to throw a banana at Mrs. Hatchett at this point. Although she did not seem so much as to glance in its direction, she gave a flickering twist with her saber and cut it in two in midair.

The pirate captain charged forward and slashed at Mrs. Hatchett, but she, with tremendous skill and a sword of razor sharpness, parried his lunge, and cut through his thick leather belt so that his trousers fell down. He dropped his sword and seized at the pants desperately, then stepped onto one half of the banana and shot across the room, winding up in a dusty corner with the classroom wastepaper basket.

"Let that be a lesson to you!" said Mrs. Hatchett majestically. "Now sit down again—and put your sword away. Your mind is about to be illuminated with literature. Of course we must start small. Open Book One. Look at the picture. I will read the first page to you. 'Look, John. Look. Look at the burglar. The burglar looks at John. John looks at the burglar. Run, burglar, run.' "

Now began a terrible time for the pirates.

16 TREACHERY FROM TOOTHPICK

The Stubborn Orphans made life very difficult for the pirates. These orphans enjoyed their classes with Mrs. Hatchett and did not like having them interrupted by a lot of ignorant pirates and a parrot. They took action at once.

For instance they detected, by mere instinct, that Toad was terrified of spiders and filled his desk with spiders of the hairiest kinds. He was often obliged to leap up and run out of the room with his hands held over his tin ears.

Then they were always setting off explosions with fireworks and dust bombs and such like—very hard on Brace-and-Bit, whose glasses were constantly being covered with soot. He had only to lift his desk lid, and *bang* ... he would be blind and blundering and covered with ashes for the next ten minutes.

Rather unexpectedly Packy proved to be his salvation. With an ingenuity one would not expect to find in a cabin boy, Packy invented little windshield wipers for Brace-and-Bit's glasses. The mere touch of soot on the lens and these sensitive wipers sprang into play and whizzed away busily, cleaning off all foreign matter.

"Very good, Packy," cried Captain Wafer in admiration. "You're pretty nearly as good as Humbert Cash-Cash when it comes to inventing."

It was hard to tell which of the orphans was the most troublesome. Annie was a dead shot at flicking pieces of paper with a rubber band, and Wolfgang was a boy who could calmly read Book Seven of the Silkweed Granulated Readers, and at the same time stick out his foot and send a pirate tumbling head over heels. Yet perhaps thumb-sucking Caramello was the worst of all. Even Mrs. Hatchett could not understand her baby babble, though she herself spoke eleven languages perfectly. What is more, Caramello seemed to have access to unlimited supplies of thumb-tacks, glue, and sneezing powder. She made the most complicated pirate traps, involving string and elastic, in a way that would have been the envy of any engineer. They certainly fascinated Packy.

"She really thinks things through. You've got to admire her," he cried, mopping Captain Wafer down, as he gasped and sneezed after one such attack.

"I don't," snapped Captain Wafer. "I'd run her through with my sword if only Mrs. Hatchett hadn't forbidden such activities. If I wasn't determined to learn reading, I'd skewer her *and* Mrs. Hatchett both, and be off to sea again."

"It could be worse," said Packy—which was easy for him to say as Caramello never, ever set traps for him.

But things did quickly become a lot worse. Something was about to happen that was exquisitely painful to the captain's piratical pride.

Dr. Silkweed came into the room one day, courtly and gracious, beaming on pirate and Stubborn Orphan alike.

"I have just had Mrs. Hatchett's weekly report on this class," he said, "and I am happy to say that there is among you a particularly outstanding pupil . . . someone who is apparently improbable, but who has a grasp of grammar and a perception of punctuation worthy of the finest instruction that this academy has to offer."

Captain Wafer tried to look modest. He was almost at the end of Book One and considered that his progress had been outstanding. Annie and Wolfgang, who were just starting on Book Seven, cast sharp glances at one another and tried to look modest too.

"Toothpick the parrot, " intoned Dr. Silkweed sonorously. "During this week, starting from scratch (I make no reference to personal habits, I assure you), Toothpick has shot ahead to Book Five of the Silkweed Granulated Readers—very propitious progress for a probationer. Toothpick—come out here, will you please."

Promptly the parrot left his perch on Captain Wafer's shoulder and landed cheerfully on Dr. Silkweed's. A hissing sound arose as all the pirates sucked air in sharply through their teeth.

"Treachery!" muttered Captain Wafer.

"No such thing," snapped Silkweed. "That pirate must stay in after school and write out a hundred times, 'I must not mutter "treachery" during class.' This delightful bird presents such promise that I shall take on teaching him myself. Oh, and by the way, Mrs. Hatchett, the police plan

70

to pop in a little later today. Something about a missing person. . . ."

So saying, Dr. Silkweed stalked out of the room, Toothpick perched triumphantly on his shoulder.

17 A Visit From the Hookywalker Police

The pirates had been deserted by their parrot—a bird in whom they had placed the utmost trust. The orphans scoffed at the idea that he could read better than they, and that Mrs. Hatchett had lost her prize pupil. Glances were exchanged.

"It's hard on a Doctor of Literature," said Mrs. Hatchett grimly, "when her reading lessons are interrupted by the police, and it's always happening here. It must be that know-it-all, Carstairs," she went on saying with bitter sarcasm, "famous for solving the mysteries of the agitated alligator and the laughing coffin."

Scarcely had she uttered these words when there came a knock on the door. Three dignified coppers entered and stood aside respectfully, as into the room strode Detective Inspector Carstairs. The air seethed as the pirates hissed again, for Detective Inspector Carstairs, though wearing the grubby brown raincoat and squashy hat that distinguish all the best detectives, had riotous golden curls and melting brown eyes. She was surely none other than the lovely woman in the photograph that Packy had carried in his pajama pocket, and that now nestled over Captain Wafer's bounding heart.* The captain turned as pale as a lily,

---

*Or over his liver, as explained previously. However, the liver is a wonderful organ and deserves nothing but enormous respect in matters of sensitive affection.

as red as a rose, then as pale as a lily once more.

"Class," said Detective Inspector Carstairs. "Class and Mrs. Hatchett! I have to inquire about the whereabouts of a missing man—none other than the well-known encyclopedia salesman, James McTodd, editor and main shareholder of the Emperor Encyclopedia Company. He was

due to sell encyclopedias among the Thousand Islands, but his ship is currently at its moorings in a suspiciously battered condition, and his sample copy of *The Emperor Encyclopedia* is missing. So far we have no trace of Mr. McTodd or his encyclopedia. His devotion to his encyclopedia was well known, and the fact that the two have gone missing together is thought to be highly suspicious. It is the duty of anyone knowing anything of McTodd's whereabouts to inform the police without hesitation."

There was silence. Then Mrs. Hatchett spoke.

73

"Is it not probable, Detective Inspector, that Mr. Mc-Todd has simply changed his mind about where the greatest need for encyclopedias lay, and has simply gone off into the country where they are always so thirsty for first-class information?"

"But someone has had his boat out," said Detective Inspector Carstairs. "It is full of footprints and fingerprints and mysterious clues. Also there were signs that someone had used it to transport what seemed to be a very large piano. We detectives can tell things like that. And not only that . . ."

She snapped her fingers imperiously and one of the policemen stepped forward and held out a little box. Then he opened it and displayed a small object held betwixt thumb and forefinger. "Take note all!" he proclaimed. "Twenty of these here clues were discovered floating in the McTodd vessel."

Winkle's jaw dropped with astonishment, Packy frowned, and little Caramello stood up to get a better view.

"Blow me down!" said Brace-and-Bit, adjusting his glasses, which he had put on upside down. "How can a piece of some old jigsaw puzzle be thought of as a clue? I'm baffled."

Detective Inspector Carstairs sighed. "I'm baffled too," she admitted. "Ten of the twenty pieces of jigsaw fit together and, on the part of the puzzle thus assembled, there is a secret formula for self-replicating raisin pudding—a formula known only to the government and Humbert Cash-Cash. If, somehow, J. McTodd has got hold of this formula we must know how and why. And if not, where is he? And how do pieces come to be floating around in his boat? I believe the answer lies within these four walls, because, floating in the bilge of the motorboat was this copy of a Silkweed Academy Granulated Reader, Book

Seven, with the name *Hermione Hatchett* stamped on its cover."

With these words her lovely eyes wandered all over the class, keenly searching for a guilty face. As she concluded her speech, her gaze met that of Captain Wafer, sitting in the front row of the class, who was trembling with such emotion that his pencil box shook. Inspector Carstairs turned as pale as a lily, as red as a rose, and then as pale as a lily again. She looked as if she might melt like a birthday candle. However, she was not a Detective Inspector for nothing. Quickly pulling herself together, she averted her eyes from the captain's adoring, copper-colored countenance, and began studying the other pirates in a very cool fashion. Suddenly the legal gaze stopped short, fixed on one particular pirate. She took a photograph from her pocket, studied it, then looked back to that particular pirate once more.

"Mrs. Hatchett!" she exclaimed, "I have reason to believe that you are harboring James McTodd in your classroom, disguised as a pirate and a pupil."

"I have no pupil of that name!" said Mrs. Hatchett calmly. "To which particular pirate do you refer, Detective Inspector?"

"That man there!" declared Detective Inspector Carstairs in tones of steel. "Constables, bring him out here so that I may question him."

The constables advanced nervously upon the suspected pirate, but they had nothing to fear. It was only Packy who was much too surprised and curious to put up any resistance whatever.

"I don't know anything about it," cried Packy as he was brought before Carstairs. "I don't remember any encyclopedias," Packy said. "I am an orphan, I think. I was found floating among the Thousand Islands in a Hookywalker

City Council packing case. I am cabin boy now, and the inventor of special windshield wipers for pirate glasses."

Detective Inspector Carstairs showed him the photograph in her hand. Packy looked at it suspiciously, holding it at all angles.

"It certainly seems to be me . . ." he began at last, in the tones of one admitting to some unattractive fact. But now Captain Wafer rose magnificently from his desk.

"What of it?" he asked. "Anyone may have an unexpected photograph. For instance—is this yours?" From under his waistcoat (more or less in the vicinity of his heart) he produced a photograph, which he held out toward Carstairs. She studied it briefly. Both she and the captain blushed deeply.

"It could be," she said at last. "But I have no recollection whatsoever of having been photographed with a hot-air balloon."

"There's an inscription on that photograph," said Mrs. Hatchett, reading over the Detective Inspector's shoulder. "It says, 'You are my sun, you are my moon, you are my own hot-air balloon.'"

"Curious," murmured Detective Inspector Carstairs. "I can't recall ever inscribing such sentiments."

Was she telling the truth? The captain had seen no glimmer of recognition in her lovely brown eyes when Packy had been brought before her. Did she really not know him (as the captain hoped), or was she simply dismissing all knowledge of both Packy and the photograph for reasons of her own? Detectives have their secrets that they must protect.

"May I ask, Captain," she said gently, "for I see by your bearing that you are the captain—how you came by this photograph?"

The captain smiled an enigmatic smile. "It is always next to my heart, madam," he said evasively, and swept her a courtly bow so deep his nose nearly scraped the floor.

"I wish you'd realize that this is a reading lesson," said Mrs. Hatchett irritably. "These pirates have much leeway to make up before they become true men of letters, and time is wasting."

Detective Inspector Carstairs became official again. "Show this man the bits of jigsaw puzzle, Robertson."

Packy looked at them, frowning. Shaking his head, he confessed at last: "They do seem to mean something to me. The same with pianos and hot-air balloons. But what they mean I just don't know."

"Look me in the eye as you utter those words," cried Detective Inspector Carstairs sternly, and Packy looked her in the eye, just as he had been told to do. A sudden expression of doubt crossed her rose-tinted countenance. "Blue eyes," she declared. "Robertson! Herring! Bogtrotter! This man has blue eyes."

The three policemen drew near to peer into Packy's eyes.

"Blue, definitely!" said Robertson.

"I'd have said more gray!" argued Bogtrotter boldly.

"Blue or gray—it's wrong either way," snapped Carstairs. "The official description of McTodd definitely states that one of his eyes is green and the other is brown." She studied Packy in amazement.

"Look at him! Identical in every respect with the said

McTodd, except for the fact that his eyes are the wrong color. How can it be?"

Brace-and-Bit leapt to his feet.

"This here Packy was fished out of the sea in a packing case full of pink-and-white tissue paper," he declared. "Subsequently it was revealed that he had lost his memory. It had gone like dew in the morning sunshine. It's shock, that's what caused it, and I put it to you that shock might cause a man's eyes to change color."

Detective Inspector Carstairs consulted her book, frowning to herself.

"It also says here," she said at last, "that McTodd had one arm slightly longer than the other. Bogtrotter, measure this man's arms."

The policeman obeyed smartly. "Madam," he said, "I have to report that this individual does not have one arm longer than the other, as indicated in the official McTodd description." There was a gasp from all except Mrs. Hatchett who looked pointedly at her watch. Packy smiled with relief.

"What he does have," said the constable meaningfully, "is one arm very slightly *shorter* than the other. It is the

wrong difference and he can't, in any way, be said to be McTodd. He seems more like McTodd's reflection in a mirror."

"Very curious, Bogtrotter, very curious indeed," said the beautiful detective. "He isn't McTodd—very well, I accept that—yet I feel his presence here means something. What was that Silkweed Academy Book Seven doing in McTodd's boat?"

"What is Mrs. Mangle's picture doing hanging up in Silkweed's study?" murmured the pirate captain.

"Why do the piano and the flamethrower seem familiar?" wondered Packy.

"Why do encyclopedias keep cropping up in our lives?" asked Toad.

"What of the Cash-Cash formula found on the pieces of jigsaw puzzle floating in the bottom of McTodd's motor boat?" pondered Detective Inspector Carstairs. "Humbert Cash-Cash came from the Deadlock Orphanage and was educated at this very establishment. I'm sure that's not accidental. And why a jigsaw puzzle?"

Winkle rose, creaking to his feet. "As to that," he was heard to waffle, "as to that jigsaw, well, I give you my word a man might find pieces anywhere. You can't rightly call them clues because they come up like mushrooms overnight." And having uttered these mysterious words, he sat down again.

"Enough!" said Mrs. Hatchett. "We must get on with our reading." And she flourished her saber.

"Indeed, we have finished our investigations for the moment," admitted Carstairs, looking forlorn. "I do not see my way clear in this matter." She sighed deeply and Captain Wafer sighed too, giving her a languishing glance. He longed to leap up, clasp her in his arms, and shower her with kisses. But you can't do that when you are halfway through an important reading lesson. Still, as she marched out of the room, he cast such a burning glance after her that it seemed it must singe the back of her detective's grubby, brown raincoat.

Mrs. Hatchett promptly fired her pistol into the ceiling to relieve her feelings, and stood sternly by while pirates and orphans meekly took out their reading books.

Only Winkle, who had not been watching Detective Inspector Carstairs, seemed agitated.

"Here!" he whispered to Toad. "Did you see what that little Caramello did back there? Blow me down, matey . . . she . . ."

"Silence between decks!" roared Mrs. Hatchett, half drawing her saber as she spoke. "Hold your whist Winkle and give Book One your utter attention."

So Winkle held his whist and Toad did not find out until much later just what it was that Caramello had done to agitate Winkle.

18   AN UNEASY CLASSROOM

The results of this day were far-reaching. Struck down both by violent love and the defection of a conceited parrot, Captain Wafer went into a melancholy decline for a day or two. Instead of shouting and swearing, he became subdued, and sat around sighing and staring into empty space.

Mrs. Hatchett was angry at having her prize pupil taken over by Dr. Silkweed as well as at having her class interrupted by the police. It made her very short-tempered, and woe betide the pupil (pirate or orphan) who forgot to stop at a period, or hesitate at a comma.

The Stubborn Orphans were upset too—mainly because Mrs. Hatchett was upset. They regarded her as the most popular Doctor of Literature in the known universe,* and they distrusted Dr. Silkweed, who was easy to distrust at the best of times.

The whole class simmered like soup, and what with one thing and another, Wolfgang and Annie took their lunches across the playground and shared their apples with Toad and Brace-and-Bit (who had nothing but ship's biscuits and tots of rum—not very appetizing really). Caramello did not join them. She had taken a great fancy to Packy, and they sat together, Caramello talking in her babbling language, and Packy nodding as if he understood, both drawing

*And probably beyond.

strange intricate pictures in the dust with pointed sticks. They could have been drawing maps of lost islands, or electronic circuits, or cross sections of plants totally unknown to science.

"We've got to watch out," said Annie. "Forces of disruption are at work."

"We must stick together," said Wolfgang. "Something is going on, and we don't know what it is."

"Toothpick would say it was doom or maybe fate," muttered Toad. "Can he possibly be right?"

"Don't mention that backsliding bird to me!" exclaimed Brace-and-Bit in disgust. "It spoils the flavor of my rum. He was supposed to be one with us, but blow me down, he's decided to be one with Silkweed instead."

Annie blew her bangs more or less out of her eyes, and said in a low voice, "Listen! I think Dr. Silkweed is trying to make Mrs. Hatchett leave the academy."

"Why?" asked Wolfgang. "She's the best teacher on the staff."

"Yes," agreed Annie, "but she's too fond of reading. When other staff members are out burgling or black mailing, she just stays at home with a good book."

"My word—so she does!" nodded Wolfgang. "She doesn't approve of crime. Gosh—suppose Annie is right? I wouldn't want to stay here without Mrs. Hatchett to teach me."

Brace-and-Bit and Toad quite agreed that Mrs. Hatchett was the shining light of the Silkweed Academy, though privately they thought that the children had got hold of the wrong end of the marlinespike.

"Take it from me," said Brace-and-Bit, "no academy in its right mind would get rid of a fine, fighting teacher like Mrs. Hatchett. I'm not worried about that."

"Nor me." Toad shook his head. "It's the captain that

goes to my heart. There he sits, a mere shadow of his former self, brought down in the world through love. What a dreadful thing it is when a man falls slave to a pretty ankle."

Such thoughts as these united Mrs. Hatchett's class. They continued doggedly with their reading lessons, for in times of stress a good book is often all the comfort you can reasonably expect to find.

19 THE MATHEMATICAL HORSE

Two days later the classroom door opened and Dr. Silk-weed, with an odious smile curling up under his dark glasses, slid into the room followed by a small, round man dressed in scarlet, with a lot of gold braid looped around him. This individual also wore his chest covered by so many gold and silver medals that he looked like a little, fat Christmas tree, twinkling and sparkling unseasonably in Mrs. Hatchett's classroom. Perched on Dr. Silkweed's shoulder was that fickle bird Toothpick, refusing to meet the scornful gaze of his erstwhile companions. Dr. Silkweed seemed as limp and languid as ever—like an un-cooked sausage—but all the same there was a slight uneasiness about him that was most unusual. A moment later something else came through the door—nothing less than a black-and-white horse, whose scarlet harness was hung all over with silver bells.

"Ah, good afternoon, Mrs. Hatchett. All happy and busy, I see," caroled Dr. Silkweed. "Good! Good! That is how it should be in the Silkweed Academy. And now—wonderful news! A new pupil! May I present Professor Fafner—a university graduate like yourself."

Mrs. Hatchett drew herself up stiffly, for there was something in Silkweed's voice that made her rigid with suspicion.

"Of what university are you a graduate?" she demanded

of Professor Fafner, narrowing her yellow eyes, like a wolf about to go for the throat.

"Oh, I am going, always, to the Hookywalker University," Professor Fafner cried, clasping his hands in a way that made her want to strike him down. "I am studying many years on the behavings of animules. It is so interesting to study the animules. I am being a great lover of animules, you know. Dogs, bears, hyenas, skunks—I am loving them all."

Slowly the orphans and pirates alike closed their books and stared hard at this little, glittering man. Never in history had there been so many narrowed eyes in the same classroom at one and the same time.

"Five years I am studying them," Professor Fafner went on triumphantly. "Five! I am becoming a five-year expert on animule behavings."

At this moment the horse did something mysterious. It bowed its head and tapped five times with its right front hoof, jingling its bells as it did so.

"Five! He is counting five, my clever one!" shouted Professor Fafner. "All the time he is counting, counting, counting. Now he is here to learn to read."

Mrs. Hatchett's yellow eyes rapidly unnarrowed and flashed like lightning. Professor Fafner and even Dr. Silkweed jumped back a pace or two.

"Read!" she exclaimed. "Dr. Silkweed—may I take it that this horse is here as a prospective pupil?"

"You may," Dr. Silkweed said. "Professor Fafner has made a lot of money with this counting horse. But he feels this is only a beginning. After all—should not a mathematician interest himself in literature too? He feels, and rightly I am sure, that the horse should get a chance to develop its abilities in a more balanced way. And besides, people will pay richly to see a horse that can read as well as count."

"So they may!" snapped Mrs. Hatchett. "But I for one must decline to be the one who teaches him. I am a graduate, sir, A Doctor of Literature from the University of Hookywalker, no less. Orphans are one thing, pirates are another. But surely you can see, Dr. Silkweed, that I must draw the line somewhere."

The Stubborn Orphans looked rather disappointed.

"Now, Mrs. Hatchett," said Dr. Silkweed winningly, "we all know that behind a gruff exterior you hide a heart of gold. You cannot intend to allow this poor horse to go out into the world illiterate. After all, you were prepared to teach a parrot."

This was hardly an observation likely to calm Mrs. Hatchett. Her hand tightened upon her saber in a very speaking fashion.

"Toothpick taught himself," she said, "and I expect he still does. I admit he is a parrot of talent. But I think it is outside of enough to ask me to teach a horse. I must decline, Dr. Silkweed."

"This Mrs. Chopper—insulting my horse, she is," cried Professor Fafner. "If parrots she is teaching, why not horses? Is it that he is having four legs, then?" The horse promptly began to tap four times. "Four legs is no disgrace. If he has only two he will fall down." The horse tapped twice. "Good money I am paying to have someone teaching my horse to read. Am I having to go to some other academy?"

Dr. Silkweed patted the agitated professor's shoulder.

"Calm yourself, dear sir," he said. "Mrs. Hatchett, as you see, this horse can already count. Why not bend a little, dear lady, and teach him to read too?" The horse tapped twice, surprising Dr. Silkweed, who pretended not to notice.

"I have eight pupils in this class, sir," Mrs. Hatchett snapped, "and eight is enough when they are as ignorant as this lot." (The horse began to tap sixteen times.)

"It is not for you to say whom you will or will not teach," Dr. Silkweed declared. "This horse stays, Mrs. Hatchett."

"Then I go!" declared Mrs. Hatchett. How magnificent she looked, defying Dr. Silkweed with a glance like lightning. "First ... pirates! Then policemen questioning my pupils, measuring one and causing another to fall in love. It is not what a Doctor of Literature expects, Dr. Silkweed, and I find it impossible to inculcate a love of reading in such an atmosphere. And now ... horses! I resign, Dr. Silkweed, from this very minute!"

Dr. Silkweed smiled a smile that caused Annie and Wolfgang to nod knowingly at each other. "Didn't I tell you!" muttered Annie, furious.

"As you will, Mrs. Hatchett," the doctor went on. "No one is indispensable. You will, in fact, be replaced immediately. The parrot, Toothpick, will take this class from now on, orphans, pirates, horse, and all."

Dr. Silkweed stalked out of the room, Toothpick, with a look of self-satisfaction repulsive in a mere parrot, still on his shoulder. Professor Fafner followed, leaving the horse behind him.

20 NEW CREW MEMBERS

There was silence in the stricken classroom for a moment or two.

"I have nothing against the horse," said Mrs. Hatchett at last, stroking the animal's nose in case its feelings had been hurt. "I am simply not convinced that it wishes to learn to read."

There were cries of despair and abuse from her class of pirates and orphans. The pirate captain, now jolted from the languid lethargy of love, leapt to his feet, once more transformed into a a ferocious bear of a man.

"Shiver my ballybonger!" he roared. "We're on a lee shore, mates! Stap my vitals if I stay here to be patronized by my own parrot! How right that sign was, back in the tearoom, where it said, 'Do not give rum to this bird.' A man who lets himself be mastered by a mere seed-eating parrot, he's a poor pooped excuse for what a pirate should be—and you may lay to that!"

Toad stood up, trembling with anger so that his tin ears vibrated alarmingly.

"Captain—let's get back to sea," he declared. "That swab, Silkweed, has sickened me of school forever."

Pushing back her bangs, Annie yelled, "I'm not staying here to be taught by Toothpick. I'm coming with you."

Brace-and-Bit bobbed up, looking thoughtful.

"I'm with you, mateys!" he cried. "But what about our

reading? How will we decipher our treasure maps? Wouldn't it be better to wait until we're on to Book Three of the Silkweed Granulated Readers—" The horse tapped three times. "Then we could be revenged on Silkweed without hesitation, and keelhaul that base bird Toothpick."

"It's an attractive proposition," began Captain Wafer, but he was interrupted by a great outcry from Wolfgang and Toad proposing that they hang Silkweed upside down in his own study, and roast Toothpick with a chestnut stuffing. What with this, and Packy loudly inventing, and Winkle whiffling in the background, Mrs. Hatchett was obliged to fire her pistol at the ceiling to restore order.

"Captain," she said, "did I hear you correctly? Are you learning to read simply so that you can decipher your treasure maps?"

"Mrs. Hatchett," declared the captain with one of his highly polished bows, "if you but knew the trouble me and my shipmates have endured through not being able to read treasure maps, you'd weep tears salty enough to pickle pork, I promise you."

"And your ship?" pursued Mrs. Hatchett. "Close at hand, is it?"

"It's in a little secret bay known only to pirates, just around the Hookywalker headland," said Brace-and-Bit, looking at Mrs. Hatchett as keenly as his dusty glasses would allow. "But we won't tell you until we know why you're asking."

"Well, I'll tell you what!" said Mrs. Hatchett, with a grim note in her voice. "I've had enough of such as Dr. Silkweed. If you're agreeable I shall come to sea with you, and teach any reading that you might happen to need. I specialized in treasure maps early in my university training before I got into the nobler aspects of literature. Just think—you will be the only pirates in history to have a Doctor of Literature as a member of your crew."

The pirates were silent for a moment, stunned with delight at the idea, for Mrs. Hatchett was not only a Doctor of Literature but a skilled hand with either sword or saber, and able to fire a pistol with the best in the land.

"Stap my vitals!" cried Captain Wafer. "Madam—you will be most welcome. This will be yet another reason for us to get into *The Pirates' Who's Who*. Besides, I for one want to move on to Book Five of the Silkweed Granulated Readers, which I see is devoted to the missing Noah's Ark Tapestry of Hookywalker—something that is a legend among pirates. We all hope to find it sooner or later, you know."

Wolfgang let out a shout.

"I'm coming too!" he cried. "I'm not staying behind. I'm going to be cabin boy."

"So am I—I mean cabin girl," declared Annie. "And Caramello can be a cabin girl too. That means bringing

91

Towelly, but it can be the ship's flag when we're washing and ironing the Jolly Roger."

"Well-er ..." said the captain, a little taken aback, "we've already got one cabin boy." And he looked at Packy only to find Caramello had scrambled onto his knee, hooked one arm around his neck, and was leaning against him, sucking her thumb in a very possessive fashion. There was no getting rid of her. "We'll have more cabin boys than any pirate ship afloat," he grumbled, "and two of them girls too." (Here, the horse, no doubt adding *two* and *too* together, tapped four times.)

"Another reason for getting into *The Pirates' Who's Who*," said Packy quickly.

"Captain, how can you hesitate?" asked Toad. "There are plenty of tea tables on board, room for everyone, and with Mrs. Hatchett, plus the Stubborn Orphans as part of our crew, *The Sinful Sausage*, will be the scourge of the Seven Seas!"

The horse began to tap seven times, as if it were applauding.

"Annie's got the best writing. She can write a note for us," Wolfgang suggested, "and we'll all sign it."

Annie wrote the following note.

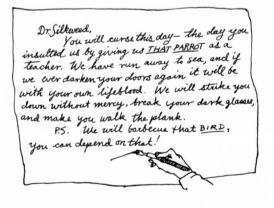

Dr. Silkweed,
    You will curse this day— the day you insulted us by giving us THAT PARROT as a teacher. We have run away to sea, and if we ever darken your doors again it will be with your own lifeblood. We will strike you down without mercy, break your dark glasses, and make you walk the plank.
    P.S.   We will barbecue that BIRD, you can depend on that!

Everyone signed this spirited epistle. The pirates wrote slowly and carefully as they had been taught; Mrs. Hatchett's signature was all loops and curls, quite remarkable. Packy took the longest to sign, as he insisted on doing a very complicated mark,* and Caramello was just as bad, as she drew a picture of a baboon.

They patted the horse good-bye, and the whole class, and Mrs. Hatchett too, sneaked out of the academy through the back door, in and out of overflowing dustbins, through an alley filled with fish heads, broken glass, and wastepaper. Within a few moments they were winding their way through the great city of Hookywalker, shaking the dust of Silkweed's villainous academy from their shoes. Although the future was uncertain, they were once again filled with hope and good cheer. Mystery, adventure, and unanswered questions seemed to sparkle in the air around them, and there wasn't one of them who did not enjoy that. Even Towelly, borne aloft by Caramello, seemed to wave in the air with a little more spirit than usual.

*Packy drew a machine he had just invented called a Weevil Mortifier. An electric current was passed through a ship's biscuit and, taken by surprise, the weevils would all drop out, shaken and hopelessly confused.

21   A Philosophical Interlude

"What a crew we've got now," said Brace-and-Bit, full of admiration for the hardy band that scuttled along the Hookywalker waterfront. "I'd like to see any witch or firedrake threaten us now."

Captain Wafer smiled rather absentmindedly. Something had just occurred to him.

"Look!" he said. "That's where *The Sinful Sausage* used to be moored during the days when it was *Ye Olde Pyratte Shippe Tea Shoppe.* How much better it is to be away from all the complexity of real life, living only by simple, romantic rules." As he said this he looked a little puzzled, as if the words were starting to ring hollow in his own ears.

"Captain—between you and me," said Brace-and-Bit, frowning, "does the romantic life seem to you to be all that simple? I mean, there seem to be a lot of unanswered questions flying about, and sometimes I get confused."

"It's funny you should say that," said Captain Wafer in a whisper, "because, to tell you the truth, it doesn't seem to me to be all that simple either." He sighed, for he couldn't help remembering beautiful Detective Inspector Carstairs, whose profusion of golden curls had made such an indelible impression on his manly heart. Brace-and-Bit guessed the thoughts that were passing through the captain's mind.

"I know, Captain, I know," he murmured. "A breaking

heart is beating within your bosom. But be strong!"

"I am being strong," said Captain Wafer pettishly. "But, oh, Brace-and-Bit—she is so beautiful! Still it can never be. I am a pirate, addicted to riotous revelry and rascality of all sorts, whereas she is a Detective Inspector, devoted to duty and defending the decrees of law and order. Our ways are set apart. Yet, if I thought I had a chance of winning her heart I would reform in a flash and lead a lawful, legal life—library cards and all—to the end of my days."

Brace-and-Bit patted the captain's arm, and they both did a bit of romantic brooding as they padded along the Hookywalker waterfront in the dusk, with catlike treads that would have marked them as pirates anywhere in the cultured world.

22 THOMAS SUMP'S JUMP

The crew of *The Sinful Sausage* had now been increased by one Doctor of Literature, one more cabin boy, two cabin girls, and a grubby, gray flag. But the crew was to be added to further still, and in the most unexpected way, before the good ship set out once more for the Seven Seas. The faithful vessel had been left moored in a bay known only to pirates, smugglers, and a few picnickers. It was drawn up alongside a long, shaky jetty that stretched far out into the bay, supported on thin, tremulous piles covered in limpets, barnacles, and other forms of marine life. Down its dangerous, tottering length crept a procession of pirates, Stubborn Orphans, and Mrs. Hatchett, loaded with bags of bananas, sets of Silkweed Academy reading books, and other necessities of life. They gained the deck of *The Sinful Sausage* with much relief, for there was something about the fragile condition of the jetty that had caused anxiety to one and all. The anchor was willingly raised, the sails were set, and with the help of a strong offshore breeze and lively pedaling from Brace-and-Bit and Captain Wafer, *The Sinful Sausage* began to move away from its moorings.

At this very moment a hoarse shout was heard and a form, strange and dim in the twilight, was seen to be charging at an unnatural speed down the jetty. Those thin and corroded piles supporting the jetty could not stand up under such thumping progress, and the jetty began to collapse behind the charging form and fall with a great splashing and crashing into the waters of the bay. Still the mystifying form kept charging on, several bounds ahead of the destruction behind it, apparently heedless of the danger it was in.

"Wait! Wait!" it shouted.

"I know that voice!" cried Mrs. Hatchett. "Thunderation! What will he do when he gets to the end of the jetty?" For *The Sinful Sausage* was drawing away from the doomed structure even faster now. Water and foam swirled angrily between the jetty and the ship, and it was hard to see how their pursuer could hope to catch up with them.

But to the amazement of all, the figure launched itself into space and, rising up in the air, leapt over the widening gap of water and landed safely on the deck, among the sun umbrellas and tea tables. It was Thomas Sump, ex-sewing teacher and piano mover of the Silkweed Academy. Thomas Sump gazed at Mrs. Hatchett and the astonished pirates (but particularly at Mrs. Hatchett) with a pleading eye, as the last piece of the jetty collapsed with a resounding splash into the swirling waters in the wake of *The Sinful Sausage*.

23 A SHORT TALE FROM THOMAS SUMP

"Thomas!" cried Mrs. Hatchett. "What are you doing here? There are no pianos in piracy, and not much call for buttonholing and slip stitch."

"Oh, such goings on!" shouted Thomas Sump. "I had to warn you! Besides, life as a pirate beats buttonholing."

"Explain yourself," said Captain Wafer sternly, and Thomas Sump did.

"There I was," he said, "practicing a bit of mouse stitch (a very tricky stitch not many sewing teachers can manage), and suddenly there was a dreadful rumpus. That parrot Toothpick was screaming that his class had run off, and Silkweed was seething because a whole set of Silkweed Granulated Readers had been stolen from the library. My mouse stitch got so big and clumsy it was more like rat stitch. The corridors were echoing with curses and criminal charges. Then I heard it!"

"What?" cried the pirates.

"I heard Silkweed say, 'Don't worry, Toothpick! They have played right into my hands. After all, valuable class sets are missing, and three promising orphans have been kidnapped, so now I've got the chance! I shall send for Detective Inspector Carstairs. I shall blame all the crimes committed by the Silkweed Academy staff on the pirates and Mrs. Hatchett. Now that they have run off they will seem to be guilty of everything, and Carstairs will be pleased to pursue them and bring them to justice. I shall even set it up so that it seems they kidnapped James McTodd and were responsible for the events on Island Six Hundred and Sixty-six, the home of Humbert Cash-Cash."

"What!" cried all the pirates and orphans, while Mrs. Hatchett fingered her saber with a grim smile.

"What events?" asked Captain Wafer in a bewildered voice. "We never even got to Island Six Hundred and Sixty-six."

"And then he said...*then* he said..." (Thomas Sump seemed anxious to change the subject) " '... I'm particularly anxious to see that pirate called Packy, for word has got around that he resembles James McTodd, and if he resembles McTodd, then he resembles a very close friend of mine whom I lost during an explosion.' "

Everyone stared suspiciously at Packy, who smiled uneasily and shrugged his shoulders.

"Well," Thomas Sump continued, "as Mrs. Hatchett knows, she is the light of my days, the red rose in the garden of my heart, the loud pedal on the piano of my dreams ..."

"Thomas!" growled Mrs. Hatchett, swishing her saber. "Careful with those metaphors!"

"Here she was," cried Sump, nimbly avoiding the saber, "surrounded by such treachery as would freeze the blood of a weasel. I knew it was my duty to warn you all that you were being falsely accused. And now I'd like to sign on with this crew, so as to be near my beloved Mrs. Hatchett."

The captain looked at him sternly.

"What qualifications do you have?" he asked. "This is a crew of wild, romantic pirates and there's little need for a piano lifter in the crew."

Thomas Sump turned his eyes aloft. "But those sails

look very tattered," he said eagerly. "As I leapt along, with the jetty collapsing after me, I said to myself, 'My word, those sails need a stitch or two!' "

"Oh, all right!" said Captain Wafer. "You can sign on as sailmaker."

So it was settled, and Thomas Sump joined the crew.

Then Packy, muttering "gingerbread," took the new cabin boy and cabin girls down into the galley while Toad and Brace-and-Bit set themselves to do some leisurely pedaling until the ship drew clear of the headland. Captain Wafer, meanwhile, showed Mrs. Hatchett and Thomas Sump the amenities of the vessel. Winkle was propped up against the wheel with instructions to watch out for rocks and whales, and while he was there, he fell to pondering on the turn events had taken.

It's very mysterious the way things are turning out, I must say, he thought, and none of 'em but me realizes how much mystification is in progress. For instance, there's those bits I keep finding and what Caramello took from the policeman. Then what about Mrs. Mangle's picture in Dr. Silkweed's study? She can't be married to him, being married to that there firedrake. And what about

Packy, floating around in that blue packing case? And the way gingerbread keeps creeping into the conversation, and Humbert Cash-Cash too. No doubt about it—something powerful, like gravity, has us in its clutches. Oh well, there's no use worrying, he philosophized.

And so saying, Winkle steered around a small whale that was basking in the warm current at the mouth of the bay and gave up philosophy as it didn't seem to be getting him anywhere.*

*It never does.

24 A Long Tale From Thomas Sump

"Well, it's been a varied day," said Mrs. Hatchett after she had admired *The Sinful Sausage* from its pedals to its sun umbrellas. "But I must retire to my cabin. I want to sort out the readers, sharpen my sword, and so on, for who knows what will happen next?"

Off she walked, swirling her Doctor of Literature gown as she went.

"Oh," cried Sump, almost dissolving with admiration, "what a woman for a mere piano mover to be allowed to worship. Oh, Captain Wafer, if only you knew the glory and anguish of a hopeless love!"

Captain Wafer thought of Detective Inspector Carstairs and sighed so deeply that Sump at once realized that he too was suffering from a breaking heart. He immediately became confidential.

"Captain Wafer, sir," he said, "may I tell you something ... something I don't dare to mention before Mrs. Hatchett? I fear I have been involved in nefarious activities, and if she gets to know of it she might strike me down in righteous anger. Now nobody wants that from the woman he loves."

Captain Wafer nodded understandingly.

"See, I didn't mention it, but I've met that Professor Fafner before," Sump said in stealthy tones, "though it was a fair while back, all of two or three weeks ago. Dr. Silkweed put it to me, knowing my weakness for moving pianos, that there was this piano that needed to be moved urgently, and he played on my professional pride by saying it would be a real challenge, even to a man like me. Well, naturally I was interested—particularly when told that this piano was over the sea. One Friday night we all climbed into the doctor's speedboat, and off we went. There was me and Professor Fafner and a lady ..."

"A lady!" exclaimed Captain Wafer.

"Well, a sort of a lady," Thomas Sump corrected himself. "She had a broomstick with her and she wore fluffy slippers—oh, and she had a great shiny medal pinned to her cardigan. The funny thing was she reminded me of Dr. Silkweed himself. Totally different of course, being female, but otherwise exactly the same. Ivy, he called her, Ivy Wangle or Dangle, I forget which."

Captain Wafer groaned eloquently.

"They began to argue at once," Thomas Sump went on, "about this here piano I had been brung along to do the moving of. 'You are too greedy, my dear Hyperion,' she

103

exclaimed (such being Silkweed's given name). 'Let's just get our hands on this wretched inventor and he'll be only too pleased to spill the beans about every last thing he knows. I didn't go to all that trouble kidnapping him when he was a mere baby in order to have him get away and go inventing and making a fortune on his own behalf.'

" 'That's all very well,' says Silkweed, 'but I understand that piano is a sort of musical computer and that our friend has programmed some of his greatest inventions into it in the form of strange melodies that can only be played on that particular piano. I'm not missing out on them. Goodness knows, even if we pack him in very carefully with tissue paper he's bound to get a bit bruised, and the shock may cause him to lose his memory. He used to lose it all the time when we had him in the Deadlock Orphanage.'

"Well she went on grumbling about me being there, taking up room, but Silkweed had his mind set on this particular piano and wasn't to be budged."

"But what was Fafner doing there?" asked Captain Wafer, already confused.

"Something to do with animals," said Sump. "It was hard for me to take it all in, but I heard wolves and baboons mentioned, and I gathered that the island we were bound for was protected by wolves and baboons. It was going to be Fafner's job to subdue them so that Silkweed and Fluffy-Slippers could slip past without being torn to pieces. But it was all mutter, mutter, mutter, and of course I was concentrating on doing a few select piano-moving exercises. You can't just walk up to a piano and lift it up without a few exercises first, you know.

"Well, at last we come to the island and a very neat, little island it was with a neat, little, blue wharf and a neat, little, yellow lighthouse on the end of it. And off they goes, loaded with sheets of pink-and-white tissue paper, and that there flamethrower Silkweed has hanging on the wall in his study.

" 'Wait a bit!' they told me, and wait a bit I did, down there in the boat, until suddenly in the profound stillness of the night, what do I hear?"

"What do you hear?" cried Captain Wafer.

"I hear another boat approaching," said Sump, "that's what I hear. A little white boat, and by the flashing light of the lighthouse I see it has words written on its side: *Emperor Encyclopedia Company* I read. Whoever was in that boat, he pulled it right up to the jetty and then got out, taking a big, blue packing case with him on one of those little trolleys that they use at railway stations and libraries and other places of culture. See—only a man with muscles like mine could have managed that packing case without a trolley."

"Of course," said the captain in breathless tones. "Go on!" He could scarcely wait to hear what happened next. But Thomas Sump *was* going on. He was so glad to be telling his story that he couldn't have been stopped with a marlinespike.

"Well, I didn't know what to do," he said. "I mean, *there* I was, and *here* was this little fellow going off up the path, and I had heard mention of wolves and baboons. Should I shout, 'Wolves and baboons!' after him just to give him a clue what he might be in for? But at that very moment there was a terrible explosion—oh, it was a night of incident I can tell you. The whole island shook, the boat shook, there were flashes of red, and ominous rumbles, and then bits and pieces fell around me like leaves in autumn, all over the boat and the jetty too. Imagine my astonishment when they turned out to be bits of jigsaw puzzle. That's not what you'd normally expect, now is it? Well, I gathered them all up as best I could and put them in my pocket. I was wearing this very jacket and—look ... here they are. ... Someone will come looking for these, I thinks to myself, because nothing spoils a jigsaw more than missing bits. Well, I'd gathered up all the pieces I could see, both in the boat and off the jetty, when along came Fafner, looking a bit flustered, I thought, and said he'd been sent to take me up to the house.

"There was a big house on that island—really quite a mansion, not that I got to see much of it, but I couldn't help noticing the doorknob, which was most unusual, sparkling away as if it was the best crystal glass. I was taken straight to a certain room with a sign on the door. *Rumpus Room,* it read. Well, I thinks to myself, as I got a gander at what it was like inside, it must have been a pretty solid sort of rumpus, for the floor was all skewwhiff, and one entire wall was missing. There was just a smoking hole, and after that nothing but a nasty, long drop down to the sea. The floor was covered with more bits of jigsaw puzzle, not to mention pages of figures, diagrams, and so on. Over against the wall was an enormous piano—a real challenge to a man in my line of business. Lying on the floor were not one, but *two* blue packing cases. I'd only seen one go in. The other must have been there already. There were bits of machinery spread around too, and among the gears and grommets and the springs and sprockets, Dr. Silkweed with Fluffy-Slippers, both looking furtive and uneasy. Things hadn't gone too well for them, you could tell that at a glance. With them was the little fellow from the boat, looking confused but excited too, like a man might look who has just had an offer of money. 'Oh Sump,' says Silkweed, very civil, but somewhat threatening (you know the way he does) ..."

Captain Wafer nodded. He knew.

" 'Sump, this is Humbert Cash-Cash, the owner of this

magnificent house, and he is anxious that we move this piano immediately. We are also taking the blue packing case with us. Help us set it up on our trolley.'

"Well, that was easy enough—the packing case was as light as a sunbeam to a man of my developments. The piano was much harder though, and when I finally hoisted it up on my shoulder I—well, I tell you frankly—I staggered around a bit."

"I understand," said the captain, afraid that Sump's embarrassment at staggering would divert him.

"I'd flexed my muscles and all that," Sump said, still brooding, "but the weight of that piano was more than enough. Well, you've seen it, for it was that very piano that is on the stage in the Silkweed Academy."

"Oh *that* piano!" exclaimed Captain Wafer, looking at Sump with increased respect. "I understand."

"If you understand, that's more than I do," muttered Sump gloomily. "Mind you, I'm a man of action and not a thinker. However, you see, in my staggering around I just happened to kick one of the two blue packing cases that was lying on the floor. Of course I was wearing my piano-moving boots at the time, and the next thing was that that there packing case shot over the floor that was sloping down toward the hole in the wall. Out it went into the starry night. For a moment we saw it shimmering against the deep blue sky, and then it was gone. A moment later we heard it splash into the sea.

" 'My samples!' cried the little man in a voice of anguish—he was a funny little chap, resembled your cabin boy, Packy, now I come to think about it. 'My precious encyclopedias!'

" 'My dear McTodd,' began Silkweed, 'that is to say, my dear Mr. Cash-Cash,' he added loudly, 'you won't need that now. Your house is filled with whole libraries of valuable books. No! Do not try to speak. I know your heart is too full for words. Take this small bag of antique gold coins I happen to have on me in payment for your piano, and we'll leave you to your inventing.'

" 'That's all very well,' said the man they *said* was Humbert Cash-Cash, though, even balancing a piano as I was, I noted that they sometimes called him McTodd by accident. 'That's all very well, but how will I sort this lot out? It looks more complicated than editing an encyclopedia.'

" 'I'll send you a trained librarian,' promised Silkweed, 'someone from my Rent-a-Librarian service. Unfortunately many of my best librarians are away stealing—I mean cataloging—rare books. But I'll send someone shortly. And now we must be gone.'

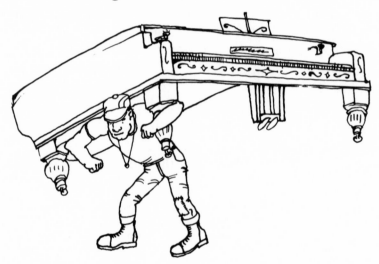

"And so off we went down the path, me staggering a bit under the weight of that piano. It annoyed Silkweed to see me stagger. I heard him say to his friend in the fluffy slippers. 'Can't you put a spell on him, to make him even stronger?'

"And she said, 'You know I don't do anything of that

sort. Of course, Mangle knows lots of spells but I'm keeping away from him at present. He'd either eat me or turn me into a firedrake along with him. Oh, how I love that man, I mean that firedrake,' she added in a snuffling voice, 'but at present he's still very hot-tempered over me turning him into a firedrake. But he'll forgive me, given time.'

" 'How much time?' asked Silkweed sourly.

" 'Oh, it'll take a while,' she replied. 'Firedrakes live about a thousand years and they don't feel they have to make hasty decisions. Still I send him a few delicious morsels from time to time. He must know I care for him very passionately. I just like getting my own way, that's all.'

"Well, we got down to the jetty and there we found our boat had sunk. Something must have fallen on it at the time of the explosion and knocked a hole in it as big as a man's head. The water had come in and the boat had gone down. I had been so busy rescuing the bits of jigsaw I hadn't noticed.

" 'We'll take McTodd's boat,' said Silkweed. 'All the better to leave him without one. He looked as if he wasn't too keen on pretending to be Humbert Cash-Cash, even though we have paid him richly.'

" 'We must remember to take that money back from him later,' cried Fluffy-Slippers. 'It was a piece of rare luck, him turning up like that—luck for us that is, not for him.'

"They thought I couldn't hear all this, though they had been talking so free before my very ears. Some people think carrying pianos makes you deaf.

" 'Soon the baboons and wolves will be waking,' cried Fafner, 'and though he is looking like Humbert Cash-Cash he is not smelling like him. These animules are relying on smell you know. He cannot escape even by swimming to another island.'

"Well, somehow we climbed into the boat and set off back to Hookywalker. Somehow we got up the path into the Silkweed Academy and put the piano on the school stage and the packing case into Silkweed's study. I was left to look after the piano. I'd never seen such a musical monster in all my life and, of course, I couldn't help being very curious about it, though I could feel, even then, I was ruined for any real piano moving in the future. My back was stretched out of all comprehensions. Well, anyhow, there I was, messing around with the piano, which had red notes as well as black ones and white ones and seven pedals too, when suddenly I saw something that made my blood run cold. The piano lid began to rise up . . . one inch . . . two inches . . . and a pair of eyes looked out at me. Horraka-potchkin! There had been someone hiding in the piano all the time."

"Who was it? cried Captain Wafer. "A wolf? A baboon?"

"No! It was that little Caramello," said Thomas Sump, looking surprised all over again. "At least, that's what I called her. You know what a one she is for hiding in pianos. Well she'd hidden in this one back on that island. Some relation of Humbert Cash-Cash, I expect. Well, I thinks to myself, I'm not letting Silkweed get this infant, and off I set to the Deadlock Orphanage because, although some people say Silkweed's at the back of it, he doesn't go there. It's run by the matron, Mrs. Tiberius. When I got there I pushed her through the After-Hours Orphan Slot they have in their door, and then I set off back to the academy. Just as well I did too, because when I got there a terrible fuss was going on. Something had gone wrong with their plans, I can't tell you what, but Dr. Silkweed and Fluffy-Slippers were lambasting Fafner and shouting at one another. He'd turned bright green all over—just a bit of spite on the lady's part I think, for she had magical powers and was lashing out with them. As for me, I cut off and hid in Mrs. Hatchett's classroom, where there was an atmosphere of calm and classical scholarship, and I stayed there until things had quieted down."

Captain Wafer sighed a world of sighs and swore, "In faith, it was strange, it was passing strange," and of course he was right too. He gazed thoughtfully at the stars, for darkness had descended. "A long story, Sump, but you have done right in confiding in me," he told the bewildered piano mover. "As it happens I have my own ideas about part of your tale, and tomorrow we'll get Annie, who's good at writing, to help us try to put the bits together, and see what we can make of it. But Sump—why not tell Mrs. Hatchett all? She is a Doctor of Literature, and besides, beneath that warriorlike exterior there beats a woman's heart. I don't think she'd run you through for any past folly if you confessed it bravely."

Sump looked uneasy.

"The thing is," he said after a moment or two, "I'm not too sure where I stand. You see I think Silkweed and Fluffy-Slippers were furious with Fafner because we'd brought the wrong packing case."

"The wrong packing case?" cried Captain Wafer.

"Yes. You see the way I had understood it was that the packing case I'd accidentally kicked into the sea held copies of a—well—of an encyclopedia, and the one we took with us contained something that required delicate handling.

But the next day, dusting Silkweed's office, I noticed that a new set of encyclopedias stamped *Sample Copy* was displayed on his shelves. Now look here, Captain, if we accidentally brought home the case with the encyclopedias in it, well, what was in the one that went into the sea?"

"What indeed?" said the captain heavily, as if he knew.

"It was me who did the kicking you see," said Sump, in a very small voice for such a big man. "I kicked it, accidental-like, but I *did* kick it, and that's not the sort of thing you want to blurt out to a scholarly lady of good, if fierce, habits, is it? Suppose, just for argument's sake, there was someone in that case; suppose for example that Silkweed was kidnapping Humbert Cash-Cash—well, he's drowned by now, isn't he? And that makes me a murderer, doesn't it?"

"Stow that gab, matey!" commanded Captain Wafer. "Tomorrow we'll get a proper grip on what's going on. Tonight, our brains need a rest, and that's a fact. Let's go and get some sleep."

25 Up and Down With the Everlasting Whirlwind

It was a calm day on the Seven Seas. Winkle was at the wheel, with Wolfgang beside him, studying maps that showed clearly all the directions they might take.

"It was to get away and lead a simple life that we put out to sea," the aged coxswain grumbled, "and things was fine and dandy for a while—for about a week. But then the captain has this idea. 'Let's steal the doorknob of Humbert Cash-Cash,' he says, and since then things have gone to pot. We've had to learn reading, the captain's fallen in love, and we're mixed up in dodgy and dangerous doings. It's just like real life all over again."

"Well, I want to go somewhere and see something," said Wolfgang, not very impressed. "Let's land on a desert island. I've always fancied a desert island."

"It would make a nice change," admitted Winkle. "I've always been fond of sand. Anything would be better than what we've got here. There's the captain and Thomas Sump and Annie under one sun umbrella, working on something that they won't let on about. . . ."

"Annie says it's a secret," Wolfgang said.

"We didn't go in for secrets in the old days—that week I was mentioning earlier," said Winkle sourly. "And there, under that other sun umbrella, Mrs. Hatchett is giving Brace-and-Bit a reading lesson. Now that's no way to run a ship. Only Toad and Packy is where they're supposed to be, and that's down in the galley."

"Where's Caramello?" asked Wolfgang. "I can see Towelly. She and Packy have run him up to the head of the mast along with the Jolly Roger, but I can't see Caramello."

"She's down in the galley too," Winkle said. "There's another thing. What man-o-war is going to take us serious as pirates, when we've got that Towelly flying aloft? It doesn't look as if we're taking piracy seriously ourselves, does it now?"

"Toad isn't in the galley," Wolfgang said. "Look, there he is now. He looks all cross."

"So he does," agreed Winkle, interested. "What's up, Toad?"

"Inventing! That's what's up!" said Toad crossly. "It's Packy and Caramello. They're inventing all over the cabin. Invent! Invent! Invent! It's all right in its place, but its place isn't in a galley. It's all much too much."

"Speaking of the galley . . ." began Wolfgang who was always hungry, but Toad swept on indignantly.

"Everything works differently from how it used to, and

now they've got this idea for inventing a machine that peels the onions for you and does the crying too."

"It sounds useful," Wolfgang remarked.

"Oh, it's useful," agreed Toad petulantly. "I say nothing against it from the point of view of *useful,* but a man can't come to terms with his gingerbread when such improvising is going on all over the galley."

At that moment Wolfgang gave a cry of delight.

"Here's one," he said. "I've found it right here."

"One what?" asked Toad suspiciously.

"A desert island," Winkle said. "He's found a desert island. Are you sure it's a desert one, Wolfgang?" He looked over Wolfgang's shoulder. "Yes, that's right," he said. "D-E-S-S-E-R-T—Dessert Island. You know, I couldn't spell a month ago," he said proudly. "What a wonderful thing is reading in a man's life. But that's no ordinary island," he added. "That's one of the Thousand Islands, that is."

"Well, can't we go there?" asked Wolfgang. "I don't feel I'll be a real pirate until I land on a desert island. And this is Island Number One."

"I'm against it," Toad declared. He shook his head and his ears wobbled alarmingly. "First there was Mrs. Mangle, and then there was the firedrake. Not to mention Packy in his packing case," he added gloomily, "which has led to a lot of wild inventing all over the ship. No—keep away from the Thousand Islands."

"I'll ask the captain," said Winkle. He seized the pirate megaphone that hung beside him. "Avast there, Captain, sir. There's members of this crew anxious to visit the Thousand Islands, notably Island Number One. What do you say, sir?"

The captain and Thomas Sump were dictating the history of Thomas Sump's adventures to Annie, with bits of the captain's adventures on Island Nine Hundred and

Ninety-nine and Island Eight Hundred and Eight-eight, and extra pieces relating to the Silkweed Academy of Literature and Languages (Dead or Alive) added.

"We'll make sense of it one way or another," the captain was growling, when Winkle's voice came over the megaphone. He leapt to his feet shouting, "No! Never! We're never going near those diabolical islands again."

"Look, Captain!" shouted another voice. It was Mrs. Hatchett, pointing with her saber. "Look at Towelly."

All eyes were raised aloft. None of them would forget what they now beheld. Towelly's color had changed. From being muddy gray it had turned a terrible blood red. It flapped about furiously though there was no wind, and the sails and even the Jolly Roger hung limp in the warm air of the Seven Seas.

The sight was so weird that pirates and orphans, Mrs. Hatchett and Thomas Sump, stood gazing at it with their mouths open.

"A most remarkable effect," said Mrs. Hatchett grimly. "I've only heard of one thing that could behave like that and I . . . but send for Caramello. She may be able to account for it."

Caramello was brought up on deck and, of course, Packy came with her. At the sight of Towelly behaving in this remarkable way Caramello began babbling away in Packy's ear, pointing and gesticulating. Packy actually seemed to understand her mysterious language.

"I think she's saying it means *danger*," he said at last. "She seems to be saying that something terrible always happens when Towelly turns red like that. It appears that Towelly is a little bit ahead of the rest of the world in time—about two-and-a-half minutes—and that, though there isn't any actual wind right now, Towelly is waving

116

around madly because there is a very big wind on the way, probably a hurricane."

Everyone stared with new respect at Towelly, which was becoming redder and redder every second.

"Towelly's actually covered in pictures," Annie said wonderingly. "I've never noticed them before."

"You wouldn't, because of the dirt," agreed Wolfgang. "It hasn't been washed for years."

At that very minute *The Sinful Sausage* gave a dreadful lurch and a sudden leap, grew still again, and then began to sigh and swing. Faithful old Winkle, still at the wheel, shouted and pointed.

Over the sea toward them came a terrifying pillar of black cloud, sea spray spinning up and up, a stem of darkness opening into a horrible blossom—a rose of angry foam, its petals twisting like propellers. It was coming straight for them.

"Oh mercy—it's the Everlasting Whirlwind," screamed Brace-and-Bit. "Oh mercy—it's got its sights on us."

And so it was, and so it had.

"Starboard, Winkle, starboard!" shouted Captain Wafer.

"Eh?" cried Winkle, who went deaf in moments of panic.

The Jolly Roger began to flap wildly, and, lower down, Towelly wrapped itself five times around the mast.

"We must be prepared to meet our ends," said Mrs. Hatchett calmly.

But Captain Wafer leapt up with a hoarse cry, seized the wheel from Winkle, and took evasive action at once—though all in vain. Wherever *The Sinful Sausage* went, the whirlwind followed, backward and forward, port and starboard, zigging and zagging across a stormy sea. Not only this, the whirlwind gained rapidly, and though Mrs.

Hatchett and Thomas Sump pedaled with all their might, the whirlwind still swept toward them with a hoarse, fearsome roar. Now they could plainly see a dark column of water filled with crabs, crayfish, seaweed, sticks, sea urchins and bits of boat from various parts of the world. Brace-and-Bit even thought he saw an admiral, all gold braid and clinking medals, being whirled around in the spiral, and Toad was certain he glimpsed a shining hot-air balloon like a bubble of sunshine. And then the whirlwind swooped and swallowed them. They went spinning, up and up, around and around. *The Sinful Sausage* behaved like a teetotum, and no one could tell up and down from back and forth, or right from wrong, anymore. All the sun umbrellas turned inside out. Thomas Sump seized Mrs. Hatchett with one arm, and Annie and Wolfgang with the other, to save them from being blown away and lost forever in the black mists of the Everlasting Whirlwind. Packy held Caramello tight and quickly tied himself to one of the tea tables. Meanwhile, Captain Wafer, showing great presence of mind, caught Winkle (who was being whisked away in an errant updraft) and hugged him tightly, though neither of them enjoyed it very much.

They went up clockwise and down counterclockwise. They rotated, they circulated, and they gyrated. They whirled and twirled and gyred and gimbled, wheeled and wallowed, and wound widdershins, and they were swept over the Seven Seas at tremendous speed—two hundred miles per hour, at least. Then, just as they were giving up hope of ever traveling in any ordinary direction ever again, the Everlasting Whirlwind grew tired of their moaning and groaning, and carelessly spat them out into a clear, green sea. As it rumbled off, spinning on its great dancing foot, the sound of sweet music reached their ears.

"Warble trout!" croaked Toad. "That's what it is. War-

ble trout! We're back there, after all. You can't deny it looks like doom and destiny, Captain Wafer, sir."

"Stow that fatalism, Toad!" commanded the captain, getting to his feet and staggering in circles in and out of the tea tables.

"Still, all the same," said Wolfgang, blinking into the clear air, "it's very funny that we should have wound up here after all."

Overhead floated a beautiful pink balloon covered with pictures of wonderful cakes, puddings, and ice-cream sundaes. On it, in letters of gold, were painted the words *Dessert Island* and the number 1 in brackets.

"A desert island at last," said Wolfgang. "Oh, Captain Wafer, sir, I vote we land on it in case the Everlasting Whirlwind comes back."

"Me too," said Annie. "Every page I wrote for Thomas Sump and Captain Wafer has blown away and I'll have to start all over again."

The captain sighed. "Oh well—since we're here ..." he

mumbled. "Towelly seems to have gone back to being gray again. Bring out the jolly boat, Coxswain Winkle."

They all rowed eagerly toward the inviting shore, and a few moments later pirates, orphans, Thomas Sump, and Mrs. Hatchett had set foot on the very prettiest beach in the Thousand Islands.

26   A Most Unusual Island

The beach of Island Number One was covered with spongy, colored sand—red, blue, yellow, green, pink, purple, orange, chestnut, chocolate, and cherry. The waves slapping at its edges resembled rainbows, and the foam lay like strings of opals left behind by an affluent tide.

"This sand looks good enough to eat," cried Annie, and to prove it she actually picked up a handful of sand and ate some.

"It's incredible!" she declared in astonishment. "It's delicious!"

"Jelly beans!" shouted Toad trying some too. "The whole beach is covered in hundreds-and-thousands."

Wolfgang ran to the little golden brown stream that flowed down into the sea, making an amber patch where it joined the green water. He stuck his finger into the stream and licked hopefully.

"It's caramel sauce!" he shouted.

Now looking around they saw clearly that the oranges on the tree to which the balloon was tied were made of orange marzipan, and the green hill on which it stood was actually an enormous cheesecake set very firm, but shaking when they all stamped their feet. The children were quite delighted and started helping themselves to pudding and jelly beans, and even the pirates, though they thought they should have minds above pudding, couldn't help trying it out too. Annie was right. It was delicious.

But the pirates were puzzled and suspicious. At any moment now, they thought, a witch might appear or even a firedrake—or something worse. They were prepared for just about anything. They wandered past a beautiful lake full of primrose yellow custard and another that seemed to consist of a vast cheesecake, garnished with whipped cream and strawberries, and then a third made of rhubarb crumb pie. Wolfgang sighed in ecstasy.

"In the Deadlock Orphanage we didn't get dessert," he said. "I used to long for dessert."

"I've never had enough dessert," Packy said. "At least I can remember that."

"Lemon meringue," Mrs. Hatchett said. "Do let me cut you a slice." And she cut slices of the lemon meringue with her trusty saber. However, by now even the orphans were feeling a little full.

"We'll come back to that later," said Annie, pushing her way past bushes that were blossoming out in little jam tarts. "Oh, Jericho! What's this?"

In front of them stood an enormous fruitcake, easily as big as a house. The path led right up to the fruitcake and there in its side, plain to see, was a door set all over with crystallized cherries and lemon peel. The pirates nudged one another.

"More witches!" they whispered. "We won't be taken in *this* time."

Yet it was a fascinating sight, and they lingered a moment staring at the cake, which was iced all over the top with white icing dribbling down the sides. A chimney, painted to resemble a piece of holly, stuck out of the very center of this remarkable edifice. As they stared, a woman came out of the door staggering under the weight of what appeared to be a roll of red-and-green carpet. However when she leaned it against the cake and began to unwind it around the cake it proved to be an enormous, frilly cake decoration.

"Somehow I never expected a desert island to be like this," said Wolfgang, scratching his head. "It's not like it is in books."

"I should hope not," Mrs. Hatchett said. "Wolfgang, I'm ashamed of you. You ought to know better than that. Thunderation! Can't you read? It was written up on that enormous balloon. It isn't a desert island. It's *dessert* island. D-e-s-s-e-r-t. We Doctors of Literature notice things like that."

"Right you are, Missus!" wheezed a new and unexpected voice. "Dessert Island it is, by both name and nature."

Out from between the jam-tart bushes shuffled an old man who seemed to be sprinkled all over with icing sugar.

"Were you thinking of making us an offer, because it's on the market, you know? It's getting a bit too much for my lady-wife and me, now that we're getting on in years.

I mean—one hot day and all your pudding's gone, for a start. It's work for a younger man. Of course, them Christmas cakes improve with age, that's why we live in one."

"Live in it!" shouted Captain Wafer. "You actually live in a Christmas cake?"

"Well, me and my lady-wife, we likes Christmas cake, you see," the old man said, rather defensively. "And when we're eating out a new room, there's the pleasure of the taste as well as the chance of finding a lucky coin. A fortune in coins went into that cake, though mind you we've got a lot of them back. There's plenty left for anyone wanting to take over, of course," he added quickly.

"How much would you want for this island?" cried Annie excitedly.

"Oh we'd want a hundred thousand something," the old man said. "Dollars or pounds or francs, or whatever you've got. But me and my lady-wife, we settled on a hundred thousand. We're getting too old for it, you see. The egg-beaters are dropping from our weary hands, and besides, we're getting sick of the witch work."

"The witch work?" cried Captain Wafer keenly. "You work for witches?"

"We do a line of prefabricated gingerbread houses for them that's too lazy to bake their own," the man said. "That's what they like—gingerbread—fortified in case the Everlasting Whirlwind comes by! There's a lot of fancy icing in a thing like that."

"What do you put in your gingerbread?" asked Toad with professional interest.

"We starts off with a hundred thousand of butter," the old man said, "and then a ditto of sugar. Then there's lot of eggs. Well, that varies. A thousand hen's eggs say, or three hundred ostrich eggs—it depends what we've got on hand. Then there's molasses...a hundred thousand of that. That's why we want a hundred thousand for the island you see. It's a figure we've got fond of over the years."

"What about ginger?" asked Packy eagerly. "How much of that do you put in?"

"Rumblebumpkin!" swore the captain. "We're men of the sea! The man that asks another question about cooking, he's the man that will feel the edge of my sword, that he will."

"We haven't a hundred thousand of anything, anyway," Wolfgang said with a sigh.

"We've got lots of courage mind you..."

"Lots of cleverness..." added Annie.

"But no money!" Wolfgang ended sadly.

Meanwhile Brace-and-Bit shoved Toad, who shoved the captain, who understood at once what they wanted to know.

"And whom might we have the honor of addressing?" he inquired, waving his feathered hat with rakish gracefulness, as pirates do, given half a chance.

The dessert maker hesitated. Then he called across to

his wife who was still struggling to put the huge frill around her Christmas–cake home.

"Mother!" he called. "Hey . . . what's my name?"

"Eh?" the old woman cried back.

"What's my name? There's someone here asking."

"You silly old man!" she screamed. "You'll be forgetting the recipe for apple pie, next. Your name's McTodd, same as mine, only you're Simeon and I'm Nellie."

"McTodd!" cried the captain, leaping as if he'd been stung. "Do you sell encyclopedias?"

"No, that's my son does that," said the old man. "My little Jim. Do you know him? Where is he? He said he'd look in on his way back, but no such luck."

The pirate captain, Thomas Sump, and Annie exchanged significant glances, though everyone else looked puzzled.

"Isn't that the one Detective Inspector Carstairs was after?" Toad asked.

"The man that looks like Packy!" exclaimed Brace-and-Bit. "Here—McTodd Senior—just look at this here individual, located by us on the bounding main, and say whether or not this is your boy, taking special note of the color of his eyes and the length of his arms."

For the first time the old man's eyes fell on Packy, who had been standing doubtfully behind the others, holding Caramello's hand. Old McTodd started, as one struck down with wonder. He goggled and he boggled and let out a hoarse cry.

"Mother!" he shouted. "Hey, Mother, here he is, found again, our little lost lad. I always knew he'd turn up someday, he was that fond of dessert."

The old woman dropped her cake frill with a shrill scream and came toward them at a wonderful pace for one so elderly.

"There's someone with good knees," Winkle muttered.

But no one else was taking any notice of Winkle.

"You mean this actually *is* your son, James McTodd?" asked the captain, already planning to restore Packy to beautiful Detective Inspector Carstairs and thereby win her heart forever.

"No, that's not Jim!" cried old McTodd scornfully. "I never said it was Jim. That's my long-lost baby son, Pakenham McTodd, stolen from his cradle when he was a little tyke of maybe two or three years by Wicked Nurse Silkweed."

"Another McTodd!" groaned Brace-and-Bit.

"Another Silkweed!" growled Captain Wafer.

"Pakenham!" screamed old Mrs. McTodd. "It *is* him, it's my little Packy!" She flung her arms around Packy's neck and embraced him warmly.

"But are you sure?" Packy said earnestly. "I don't deny it. . . . I can't deny it. I can't remember one way or the other. You see I was found a while ago, floating in a packing case, and since then my memory's been on the blink. Was I stolen?"

"When you was two!" cried the happy mother. "Two years of age that is," she added quickly.

"Where have I been since then?" Packy looked more confused than ever. "Are you sure I'm it? I mean, that it's me?"

"Of course I'm sure," declared the old woman. "A mother's heart always knows her little one. And then, no doubt, we can prove it by your tattoo."

"My tattoo?" Packy hesitated only a moment, then began to pull off his sweater and unbutton his shirt.

"A secret recipe for gingerbread in four verses," old McTodd said proudly. "We had it tattooed on him in infancy. It was to be his legacy, you see. I always thought that wicked Nanny Silkweed stole him to get her hands on that recipe."

"Nonsense, Dad," cried Mrs. McTodd. "It was because she wanted him to help her brother get that orphanage of his started. They had the building and the matron. All they needed were some orphans. We found that out years later."

"Packy's tattoo!" cried Toad. "That's right! He *is* tattooed on his chest, and in the excitement of learning to read I'd forgotten all about it. We couldn't read it, you see. But this is Mrs. Hatchett, a well-known Doctor of Literature. Maybe she could read the tattoo for us."

"Fortunately, once I had majored in treasure maps, I *did* do a unit on tattoos," Mrs. Hatchett said. "I think I can undertake to read a tattoo on any part of anyone without making any undue error, or causing embarrassment."

Packy had torn his shirt open, and several columns of the fine print were now revealed.

"Thunderation! That's no recipe! That's an epic!" cried Mrs. Hatchett. "You said four verses."

"It *was* four," McTodd said. "We would have put more, but his chest was so small in those days."

"There are seven verses here," said Mrs. Hatchett. "Four red and three blue. Packy, do you give me your permission to read these verses aloud? There may be lines here that are deeply private and personal."

"Nothing's private to a man with no memory," Packy

replied. "Fire ahead, Mrs. Hatchett. Let me know the worst."

"She will," promised Thomas Sump proudly.

And Mrs. Hatchett did.

> *Of butter take three ounces*
> *And the same of sugar too.*
> *Heat gently till it's melted*
> *To a sort of sticky glue.*
> *An egg must then be beaten in—*
> *(Of seagulls' eggs, use two!)*

"Quite right so far," declared old McTodd, beaming with pride.

> *Three ounces, next, of wheaten flour,*
> *Now add a cup of ginger.*
> *The mixture will be very hot,*
> *A culinary singe-er.*
> *But though it's bound to make you glow,*
> *It won't exactly injure.*

"It was for arctic explorers and Eskimos, you see," old McTodd explained. "Normally that amount of ginger would strike a maddened bull down in its tracks, but things is different in polar zones. That's what they call geography, you know."

> With milk and soda mixed with fruit
> The mixture is extended,
> A blessing for the Eskimo
> For whom it is intended.
> And those who're doubled up with cold
> Will quickly come unbended.

> You scientists whose constant search
> For knowledge leads you forth
> To mountaintops or polar shores
> (The South Pole or the North),
> This gingerbread could save your life
> From subantarctic wrath.

"That's where our tattooing finished," Mrs. McTodd said, but there was more to come, and Mrs. Hatchett read on.

> When Lapps or bold Alaskans fall
> Victims to icy ill,
> A slice of Cash-Cash gingerbread
> Restores them with a will,
> And makes them smoulder in the snow
> And saves them from the chill.

"Cash-Cash gingerbread!" cried McTodd in a furious voice. "What does it mean, Cash-Cash gingerbread? That's *my* recipe."

"There's an inventor swab by the name of Humbert Cash-Cash who's made a fortune selling gingerbread to Eskimos and such," Toad told him. McTodd began to go purple, a dangerous thing for a man of his age, and Mrs. Hatchett read on rapidly:

Hooray for Cash-Cash gingerbread!
That challenges and cheer-ohs!
Explorers, skiers, mountaineers . . .
The gingerbread of heroes,
That lights the heart with glowing fires
Outglowing even Nero's.

However in the temperate zone
The very merest portion
Must be approached with great respect . . .
Pray—take a crumb with caution.
And in the tropics it can lead
To heat shock and distortion.

"What beautiful reading!" cried Thomas Sump.

"Yes, lovely!" agreed Winkle. "It's a long time since I listened to any poetry, and it's done me good. My knees feel more bendable. What a wonderful thing poetry is." But nobody was taking any notice of Winkle.

The pirate captain looked at Packy sternly.

"How is it that Mr. and Mrs. McTodd invent a recipe for polar zone gingerbread, and Humbert Cash-Cash gets all the credit?" he said. "If you are the [long-lost] Pakenham McTodd, who added the extra verses with the ever-recurring name of Cash-Cash mentioned in them? How?"

"Yes, how? And who?" asked the bewildered McTodd.

"How can I tell how or who?" cried Packy in exasperation. "Heaven help me, I haven't a clue."

"I'll tell you," declared a solemn voice that was mystifyingly familiar. "It's destiny, that's what it is. Doom and destiny!" There, perched on a jam-tart tree was a bright green parrot—Toothpick, no less. "That man there," he cried, "plucked from the cerulean surges of the savage sea in a packing case is none other than Humbert Cash-Cash himself!"

27 AFTERNOON TEA AND REMINISCENCES

But Toothpick appeared a pathetic parody of a parrot, his little head bald on top, and his tail a mere travesty of what a tail ought to be. There was something so dejected about him that the captain hesitated to run him through with his sword, richly though the bird deserved it.

"Do you know this fowl?" asked old McTodd, looking at Toothpick with astonishment.

"Foul's the right word," said Toad. "It's a long and painful tale."

"It does look painful," agreed Mrs. McTodd, looking at Toothpick's tail.

Tears trickled from Toothpick's round eyes, a sight both rare and moving, for parrots seldom cry.

"Look," said Mrs. McTodd, "how about a cup of tea all around? It sounds to me as if there's a lot of explaining to be done, and there's nothing like a cup of tea and a few jam tarts to dispel confusion."

"If you bring the jam tarts I will make the tea," promised Toad. "The deck of our ship is covered with tea tables and sun umbrellas. It'll be just like old times."

It *was* just like old times, and there was a wistful expression in the captain's eyes. Just for a fleeting moment the longing to be a tea-shop man once more ran like fire in his veins. It had been such a simple life in spite of taxes, library cards, and telephone bills. Being a pirate was beginning to depress him a bit. There were so many details that needed attention. Lifting his eyes aloft with a nostalgic sigh, he observed the golden balloon hovering a little to the southeast, and caught the glimpse of someone with a telescope. However he didn't take much notice. He was getting used to seeing it around.

They got down to business at once, trying to work out just who Packy was.

"He was such a pretty baby, and we was that proud of him, you'd have thought he was a baked alaska turned out perfect," declared Mrs. McTodd. "We even got him a nanny," she went on, beginning to snuffle. "We was both so busy, and we didn't want our little one neglected. Ivy Silkweed she was called. She was quite pretty, but she had a wicked heart."

"Her brother was just as wicked as she was," went on McTodd hastily. "His name was Hyperion Silkweed, and he was starting off in the orphanage business—the Deadlock Orphanage. His idea was to get together a group of talented orphans who would be so grateful to him that they'd work for him and his rascally schemes day and night."

"Well, Ivy Silkweed was very taken with our little Pakenham," said Mrs. McTodd. "Only natural really. He was inventing already. His first invention was at the age of two: a special birthday bubble pipe that blew bubbles of sparkling lemonade. To this day I don't know how he did it."

"If only I could remember," groaned Packy. "Go on."

"Well, we got home from our dessert laboratory one day and found ... and found ..." McTodd's voice trembled.

"Wicked Nanny Silkweed had run off with our little Packy," wept Mrs. McTodd.

"We didn't know about the Deadlock Orphanage then or we'd have gone there at once." McTodd had got com-

134

mand of his fine old features again. "We searched and scanned, pried and pursued—but all to no avail. Our little Pakenham had vanished off the face of the world and so had Ivy Silkweed."

"She married a magician who was called Mangle, actually..." Brace-and-Bit began, suddenly realizing what must have happened, but McTodd was too caught up in his tale to listen.

"And then I thought of desserts. Our little Pakenham was crazy about his desserts," he cried. " 'Why, Nellie,' I said, 'if we make our island over with desserts, sooner or later little Pakenham will beat a way to our door.' "

"And he was right, wasn't he?" cried Mrs. McTodd, beaming through her tears at Packy, "because here you are, bigger and better than ever and with three extra verses as well," and she gazed at him fondly, pressing strawberry shortcake into his hands.

"I only wish I could remember it," Packy sighed. "Of course, I always have been very fond of dessert, but..."

"And then we had our Jim," Mrs. McTodd went on. "He looked much like Packy, except for his eyes, but he was a totally different case, wasn't he, Dad? No inventing for him. He was strong on memorizing." (Packy groaned in jealous anguish.) "He could remember everything he ever heard and a lot of other stuff as well. 'Why Jim,' I said to him, 'you're a little encyclopedestrian,' and so he was too. He grew up to sell encyclopedias. First he'd write them, then he'd sell them. He was on his way to Island Six Hundred and Sixty-six where some rich man lived, to sell encyclopedias there, and he said he'd look in on the way back. But we haven't seen him since. I've been expecting his little launch to come in any day and see him pushing his trolley full of encyclopedias in a blue packing case up between the custard and the cheesecake, but so far—nothing."

Thomas Sump gave the groan of a man tortured with guilt, but no one noticed.

"And meanwhile, this parrot is trying to make out that Packy is not only Pakenham McTodd but Humbert Cash-Cash too," Captain Wafer said thoughtfully. "Of course you can't believe a word he says, but we might as well take another cup of tea aboard and listen to whatever lying tale he has to tell."

28 TOOTHPICK'S TALE

Toothpick was already looking a lot better. Clutching a jam tart, he now began to talk in a low, querulous voice very unlike his usual sharp tones.

"You see before you a bird stricken with remorse, a bird anxious to eat humble pie as well as jam tarts, a crestfallen prodigal."

"He's never ever had a crest," growled Brace-and-Bit.

"I have been brought low by Silkweed—the serpent, Silkweed, the wolf in the grass, Silkweed, the snake in sheep's clothing," Toothpick continued, and would have gone on abusing Silkweed for some minutes if Mrs. Hatchett had not drawn her saber and said to him, "Toothpick, stop mixing your metaphors!" in a voice so threatening that the parrot went on hastily.

"Oh, I was promised a class to teach and power beyond the wildest dreams of most parrots, but my class ran off and it seemed my brilliant career would come to nothing.

" 'Never fear!' said Silkweed the swindler, 'you shall rise to even greater glory. You shall be a librarian and work for my Rent-a-Librarian Book Burglary business.' Well, by then I was so puffed up with conceit and vanity I agreed.

" 'We have work for you on Island Six Hundred and Sixty-six,' said Silkweed, the double-dealing doctor of deceit. 'Humbert Cash-Cash lives there, and he is a very absentminded inventor. His books are full of scrips, scraps, and diagrams that he has misplaced, and it will be your job to go through his vast library and sift these out. Research we call it, but I think you will be up to it.'

"So far so good, but when I mentioned the matter of payment for my valuable services, the doctor went black with fury, clapped me into a cage, locked the door, and delivered me into the care of that humbug Fafner. That was when my castles in the air began to crumble. Alas, alas for vain ambition."

"Get on with it, Toothpick," said Captain Wafer, though he couldn't help feeling a little bit sorry for the wretched bird.

"Off we set in a helicopter," Toothpick went on, "and soon we were circling over Island Six Hundred and Sixty-six, and the magnificent mansion of Humbert Cash-Cash was spread below us. The island was well guarded by wolves and baboons that howled and chattered at us as we flew over, particularly when they saw Fafner was piloting the helicopter. They obviously detested him, but of course in the helicopter he was quite safe, and we simply flew in at the side of the house where there was a big hole, as if a bomb had gone off in one of the rooms there.

"A man was waiting for us, and I saw at once he looked just like Packy there, apart from some trifling differences in the length of his arms and the color of his eyes, and I was told that this was the famous inventor, Humbert Cash-Cash.

"What rubbish! How could it be? That man had no feeling for inventions at all. He couldn't work a can opener. A simple snap fastener was far beyond his capacities. No way could he have been a famous inventor! Besides he didn't know his way around the place. He was always walking through some door, smack into a revolving wardrobe, or a cupboard full of jam. No! He was a mere puppet, kept there to make people think that Humbert Cash-Cash was in residence. His job was simply to answer the phone and help me with sorting through the library books, looking for notes and diagrams."

"Did many people telephone?" asked Captain Wafer curiously.

"Well, that snoopy Detective Inspector Carstairs was always on the phone," Toothpick said. "She said it was part of her official duty to check up on him."

A gritty sound like a pepper mill grinding small stones was heard under the sun umbrella. It was Captain Wafer's teeth grating together with jealousy.

"She used to ask him about little Nell," Toothpick went on. "That threw him. He had no idea about anyone called Nell and didn't like to speak out boldly in case he said the wrong thing."

"That's very strange," said Mrs. McTodd. "My name's Nell."

There was a sudden disturbance. Caramello had jumped

up, waving her arms and talking in her own babble to Packy.

"She says her name is Nell too," he said in a puzzled voice.

Thomas Sump, Captain Wafer, and Annie stared from Mrs. McTodd to Packy to Caramello. It was just possible to imagine that, if Caramello had been Mrs. McTodd's age, or the other way around, they might have looked very much like one another.

"Get on with your story, Toothpick," said Brace-and-Bit. "There must be more to come."

"Well, I got friendly with the so-called Humbert Cash-Cash," Toothpick said. "We were companions in misfortune. We were locked in the library, confronted with thousands of books—as many books as there are grains of sand on the seashore, or stars in the sky...."

"Stow the poetry," growled Captain Wafer.

"But there was a huge jigsaw puzzle on the table there, partly done, the rest scattered all over the place. It showed all sorts of interesting pictures—there was a whole school scene, recipes and gadgets, an air balloon, and part of what seemed like a wedding picture. Well, pretty soon we were hooked. We couldn't leave it alone. We kept trying to put more of the puzzle together instead of looking through the books, as instructed. Fafner was always there, trying to boss us, shouting and cracking his whip—he referred to me as "Polly," so that shows you what a cruel tongue he had. But really he was lazy. He just wanted to get back to the comic book he was reading. He kept pulling my tail feathers out to mark the place. So we went on with the giant jigsaw, while my companion told me his life story in a whisper.

"Just as you might imagine, he was the missing encyclopedia salesman, Jim McTodd. He was a victim of Silk-

140

weed's silvery tongue, just as I was. He wasn't sure what had happened to the real Humbert Cash-Cash, but he'd been told that he'd exploded himself, and he'd believed it, because, as he had gone up the path with his case of encyclopedias there had been a big explosion, you see. He'd agreed to stay on the island to pretend to be Humbert Cash-Cash since Silkweed had pretended to be a detective inspector and had asked him to protect the plans and inventions from spies and enemies. Mind you, almost at once he'd had his suspicions."

"Why?" asked Captain Wafer keenly.

"Well, because Silkweed stole a piano. Jim said a great piano-moving giant was brought in, and he actually picked up this piano and walked out with it. A huge chap, Jim said, and out of spite he'd kicked the case full of encyclopedia samples into the water before he left."

"Lies!" cried Thomas Sump. "It was an accident."

Now, all eyes, including Mrs. Hatchett's, were turned in his direction, and he began to glow like a potbellied stove, and duck his head for shame. Guilt was written on every one of his homely features.

"Be that as it may," said Toothpick, "I thought things over and I came to the following conclusion. We know that Packy was pulled out of the sea in a blue packing case and that there is, at this very moment, a set of sample encyclopedias in Silkweed's study. What I think is that Silkweed set out to kidnap Humbert Cash-Cash and had him all packed up with pink-and-white tissue paper, but someone—I name no names—accidentally kicked the said Humbert Cash-Cash into the sea, and all Silkweed got were the sample volumes. Meanwhile, we noble pirates come along and rescue the floating inventor, christening him Packy because he'd lost his memory and because he was found in a packing case."

One and all agreed this was a very convincing reconstruction of events.

Mrs. Hatchett marveled. "How clear it's all becoming now. Packy, you must have run away from the Deadlock Orphanage and set up business as an inventor, using the gingerbread recipe you have tattooed on your chest."

"I never dreamed a life of romance would be so complicated," groaned Winkle.

"Packy and Jim are brothers," cried Brace-and-Bit. His glasses had gone all steamy with emotion. "That's why they look so strangely alike!"

"A brother!" cried Packy. "I have a brother. And my little brother is a prisoner of Silkweed. My little brother whom I've never met." He glared at Toothpick. "Why did you leave him there? How did you escape?"

"One of the baboons—a fine intelligent beast—threw a stone at Fafner and broke a window. It was only a small hole but I was out of it in a flash," Toothpick explained. "'Go!' Jim shouted after me, 'Go and tell the world my story!' and that is what I've done. All is explained."

"Not quite, I think," said Mrs. Hatchett. "Thomas, how did you come to be on Island Six Hundred and Sixty-six, stealing a piano?"

"Oh, have mercy, Mrs. Hatchett," cried Thomas Sump, writhing in agony before the woman he adored. "I have suffered the perpetual anguish of remorse."

"Speak up, Sump," cried Captain Wafer, striking the abject piano mover on the shoulder. "Don't shiver and shake! Mrs. Hatchett has a tender heart. She will understand that you are a mere victim of circumstance."

"That's as may be!" said Mrs. Hatchett shortly, testing the edge of her saber with her thumb, but when she heard his tale her stern face softened. "Silkweed shall pay for this. He has led you into wicked ways. His grammar is good

142

but his morals are bad. He shall pay for this!"

"Yes!" cried Mrs. McTodd. "He stole our little Packy—
revenge on Silkweed!"

"Revenge on Silkweed," boomed Captain Wafer.

"Revenge on Silkweed," chorused the crew and the orphans.

"Revenge on Silkweed!" repeated Toothpick with relish.

The Sinful Sausage, powered with so many good pedalers
and by much-improved sails (Sump had edged them with
a herringbone stitch, which he thought suitably salty), shot
out of the harbor of Island Number One at a tremendous
rate, and within twenty minutes Dessert Island was deserted.

29 ISLAND SIX HUNDRED AND SIXTY-SIX—AT LAST

Packy and the orphans went down into the galley to help Toad. Packy had to stand with his shirt open while Annie read his recipe aloud, and Wolfgang and Caramello made a batch of Cash-Cash polar-zone gingerbread out of the purest intellectual curiosity. Toad made conventional pirate gingerbread that was much milder (though still very hot).

Meanwhile, working between them, and under them, and over them, the McTodds put together a picnic lunch, nutritious and sustaining, as suited such an occasion.

Never had a ship looked as deadly and determined as *The Sinful Sausage*, slip-slipping between the Thousand Islands, accompanied by a whole choir of warble trout. Of course, with Mrs. Hatchett and the orphans on board there was no chance of mixing up Island Six Hundred and Sixty-six with Island Nine Hundred and Ninety-nine.

They passed many islands, all different, all beautiful, but the children, reading the numbers on the bright balloons that bobbed against the blue skies, shouted the numbers aloud, and even the pirates were able to join in a bit, though their reading and counting still had a long way to go.

Although there were so many balloons the most interesting and beautiful of all was the one that rode high in the air, golden and remote as a doubloon, or a single piece of eight in a pirates' dream.

"What balloon is that?" Annie asked.

"Oh, it's not attached to any island," Toad told her. "It's out on its own, and it follows us around. I think it likes us."

At last, one island more beautiful than all the rest began to rise out of the sea, like a green bun puffed up with magical yeast. It was an island that was a microcosm of the whole world, with forests and gardens and beaches, and little deserts, and cliffs and streams and caves and waterfalls, and on the very top of it was a house rather like a castle, but more homely. Pelicans and flamingos flew overhead, the sands were shining silver, and there was the little blue jetty with the yellow lighthouse on the end of it, just as Thomas Sump had described it.

They drew up beside the jetty and cast anchor in the crystal waters. Immediately a pack of wolves, all howling savagely, poured out of caves on the foreshore, and a large band of belligerent baboons trooped down from among the rocks and squatted on the shore, baring their yellow teeth and scratching themselves in a way that boded ill for anyone who tried to set foot on the silvery sand.

Captain Wafer turned to Mrs. Hatchett. "Suppose you take the baboons, ma'am, and I tackle the wolves?"

"Do remember!" said Toad anxiously, "they're very rare, those wolves! They're a protected species."

"I'll remember that they're a protected species if they remember that I'm one," said Captain Wafer with some asperity, while Brace-and-Bit, thinking he was about to witness appalling bloodshed, quickly took his glasses off and faced the wrong way.

But Caramello leapt up onto the jetty and ran along it at great speed. It was just as if she were on her way to meet old and well-loved friends.

"Caramello's had it," said Wolfgang desperately.

But when Caramello arrived on the shore, the wolves leapt around her like puppies while the baboons danced in a ring around her. It was obvious to all she was loved by baboons and wolves alike. There were squeaks and grunts and barks of delight.

"Listen to that," said Annie. "This explains a lot. Caramello can talk animal language. She's explaining to them who we are."

A moment later the whole crew, with Toothpick on the captain's shoulder as of old, advanced down the jetty, pushing the reluctant Packy forward. After all, those wolves and baboons were probably *his* wolves and baboons, and a man ought to be able to keep his own pets in order. As it turned out, the wolves and baboons were just as delighted to see Packy as they had been to see Caramello. The whole crew was permitted to cross the beach and to climb the great staircase that led up the steep side of Island Six Hundred and Sixty-six to the wonderful house on the top.

30   THE CAPTURE OF FAFNER

"More stairs!" groaned Winkle. "This is the second time we've had stairs on these islands. It isn't fair to a man's delicate knees to have to go up and down like a yo-yo."

But Packy smiled and pressed a button. There was a creaking and grinding and the staircase shook all over like a wet dog. Then it began a grumbling but steady ascent, carrying pirates, orphans, Mrs. Hatchett, Thomas Sump, and the McTodds right to the top of the island, toward the very front door with that very glittering doorknob.

"I wish I'd known about that button when I was carrying the piano," Thomas Sump declared, quite riven with wonder.

"I'm glad I remembered it," said Packy. "My memory is coming back now, in bits. The farthest memories are clearest. I can remember my miserable childhood in the Deadlock Orphanage, with nothing between me and despair except my inventions. I can remember Dr. Silkweed praising me for inventing a flamethrower..."

"That very flamethrower he has hanging in his office to this day!" declared Brace-and-Bit rather reproachfully.

"It was! It was!" cried Packy, in an ecstacy of remembrance. "When I saw it there it stirred something in my poor, battered memory, but I couldn't quite latch onto it at the time."

At that very moment the staircase quivered and stopped

right outside the Cash-Cash door and there, glittering with icy fires, was the Cash-Cash diamond doorknob, so much more beautiful than a mere lemon drop that tears ran out of Brace-and-Bit's eyes at the sight of it. Everyone looked at Packy in admiration, and he glanced around modestly, saying, "Oh well—it's nothing really, just a lump of carbon crystallized in regular octahedrons." (After all, there is no use in knowing that sort of thing if you don't tell other people occasionally.)

But the pirates were not interested in the diamond now. They were mad for revenge. When they found the door was locked, the captain banged on it angrily, and Packy rang the doorbell—which did not ring but coughed three times in an important voice. Faint at first and then more and more loud, they heard the sound of feet approaching down an echoing hall. A moment later an unpleasant voice, well remembered by all, was heard asking at the keyhole:

"Is it you that is coughing on the bell, Hyperion?"

At the sound of that voice Mrs. Hatchett could hardly wait to draw her chopper.

"That fat little phony! I'll give it to him!" she cried, and shivered the door with two hacks of her saber.

All present, peering through the hole, saw the fat figure of Fafner hurtling down the hall as fast as his small legs would carry him. Thomas Sump soon overtook him, seized him by the collar, and whirled him off his feet, where he hung screaming and kicking with despicable cowardice.

"This way," shouted Toothpick. "I know just where we are." And off they went, taking their prisoner with them, through a maze of passages filled with bookcases, harps, pinball machines, giant ferns, stuffed warthogs, football players in frames, motorcycle gear, and glass cases filled with rare shells, coins, stamps, and medallions—the fruits of a youthtime of collecting.

"It's wonderful how it all mounts up," cried Packy proudly, staring at his collection with tears in his eyes. Now that he looked afresh on the stuffed warthogs and pinball machines he was astonished to think he could ever have forgotten them.

"Jim!" shouted Toothpick, fluttering overhead. "Jim! Here we come. It's me, Toothpick! Help and rescue is at hand. Come on everyone. Here's the library."

31   JIGSAW MANIA

They all crowded into a vast room lined with shelves and shelves of books. Over the huge hole in one wall Silkweed and Fafner had fixed a net. There was a wonderful view of the sea and the Thousand Islands through the big hole, like a view from a cliff with a steep drop below. The floor was slightly tilted, but after days at sea that seemed natural to everyone. Running down the center of the room was a table as big as a tennis court, covered in jigsaw patches and pieces, behind which rose a figure that all saw to resemble Packy exactly—except for having one eye brown and one eye green.

"Oh Jim, my baby!" cried Mrs. McTodd, casting herself upon him as a billowing wave casts itself upon the firm and friendly sand.

"Mother! Father!" exclaimed Jim McTodd (for it *was* he), trying to hold his mother up by one hand, and give his father the firm, manly, honest handshake of an encyclopedia salesman with the other.

"James McTodd, I presume," said the pirate captain, and the pirates nudged one another thinking that it was a greeting that would go down in history.

"Brother!" exclaimed Packy. "My long-lost little brother that I never knew."

"No—*you* were the long-lost one," Mrs. McTodd cried, irritated to hear him getting it wrong.

"Humbert Cash-Cash!" cried Jim McTodd. "You must be Humbert Cash-Cash, inventor *extraordinaire,* owner of this splendiferous mansion."

"He is Humbert Cash-Cash," Mrs. Hatchett agreed. "But he is Pakenham McTodd as well, stolen in infancy by Miss Silkweed (sister of the doctor of that name, and now Mrs. Mangle, a noted witch), and restored to you by the efforts of these noble pirates and equally noble orphans."

"Not to mention the noble parrot," put in Toothpick.

"Brother!" exclaimed Jim, catching on quickly.

"Brother!" cried Packy, and they embraced each other with true fraternal fervor, patting each other on the back in a way that went to the heart of all observers.

"And now let's be gone," cried Jim, "for at any moment Silkweed and his gang could burst in on us. He plans to return by boat today and strip this island of everything valuable on it, even and especially the diamond doorknob. Let's go quickly to Hookywalker and get the police before he comes back."

The captain, as can be imagined, was just as eager as Jim to fetch the police, but his crew was paying no attention. They were clustered around the patches of jigsaw puzzle, which seemed to be made up of hundreds of pictures like a comic strip.

"Look!" cried Wolfgang. "Here's your gingerbread recipe again, Packy!"

"Look!" cried Annie. "Here's you escaping over the wall of the Deadlock Orphanage by catapult!"

"Look!" cried Brace-and-Bit. "The flamethrower!"

And Winkle, Thomas Sump, and Caramello were emptying their pockets of the pieces they had found or stolen and saved, and were all agog to see where they might fit.

"Shiver my sides!" roared the captain. "Have you forgotten *Revenge on Silkweed*?! Packy's pictorial lifestory must wait!"

"Look! This looks like Packy's wedding," said Thomas Sump in envious tones, casting a languishing gaze at Mrs. Hatchett.

"What! Where?" exclaimed the captain, pushing the others aside to look closely at the picture of Packy's bride. Could she be Carstairs, whose photo Packy had had in his pocket when rescued? Was she like Carstairs at all? Packy was there, complete, but his bride had a piece of her chin missing, and the golden curls, if there were any, were concealed beneath the bridal veil.

"Who is your wife, Packy? I must know the truth!" cried the captain with feeling.

"If only I knew!" groaned Packy in an anguish of frustration. "My memory of the recent past still escapes me. My childhood days are an open book—but as for the rest..."

"We can't go into all that now!" interrupted Jim McTodd desperately. "We've got to be gone!"

Packy turned to his brother. "But this puzzle is bound to help bring my memory back. I can't leave here without knowing what happened to me. And look, here are descriptions of inventions—secrets that Silkweed is longing to possess."

"Then shove the whole puzzle in a packing case and bring it with you," said Jim, but this caused a cry of outrage from one and all.

"Break up what's already done? Never!" The jigsaw had them well and truly in its thrall, something that everyone dedicated to jigsaws will understand.

Jim had lost his only ally: The captain was hunting more feverishly than anyone—hunting for a piece of a pretty chin.

"It will take quite a time..." conceded Packy, wavering.

"On the other hand," said Mrs. Hatchett calmly, "there are a lot of us, and some of us are very intelligent. Don't panic, Pakenham. We'll all pitch in and you'll soon have your memories and inventions back."

Professor Fafner, lashed securely to a marble column, sneaked a look at his watch and gave a nasty, snuffling giggle. He was obviously delighted that they were not rushing off to sea immediately.

So the work went on with a will. The pirates displayed a single-minded concentration that was nothing short of amazing in persons used to the to-ing and fro-ing, and coming and going, in a tea shop or a ship at sea. The busy

154

silence was broken every so often with a cry of triumph as one island of jigsaw was connected to the next.

"Here's Packy after running away from the Deadlock Orphanage. See? He went to live in a very cheap attic in a seedy part of the Hookywalker waterfront and ate nothing but porridge for a year."

"Here he is baking his first batch of Cash-Cash gingerbread for the Grumbarton South Pole Expedition, and here he is opening his first bank account."

"Here's that beautiful hot-air balloon," said Annie. "So that's something to do with you Packy! I did wonder. It seems to follow you around like a faithful dog."

"Ah, this picture of lightning piercing through a thundercloud . . ." said Packy. "That was important, I do know. And some bars of music beside it . . ." He hummed a few notes but they didn't jog his memory, so he went on searching among the pictures for something that would.

Even Jim, Fafner noted with satisfaction, was totally engrossed in the jigsaw.

As the pictures grew and the piles of unattached pieces shrank, it became clear that some of the gaps would never be filled—the bride's chin among them.

"Some bits fell in the sea," sighed Thomas Sump. "I couldn't get those. The waves swooped them away."

"Vital sections are lost," said Mrs. Hatchett, "but no one is to blame." Thomas's looks spoke his gratitude for this magnanimous acquittal.

Winkle made a creaking, crackling sound—the old pirate was laughing.

"You wouldn't have done even this much if it hadn't been for me. I knew those bits and pieces would come in handy," he crowed. "Not everyone would have bothered, but I did. I gathered them up on Island Nine Hundred and Ninety-nine, and I gathered them up on Island Eight

Hundred and Eight-eight, and I got them out of Packy's packing case. Then I got some more off the carpet in Dr. Silkweed's study—very suspicious, I thought—*and* I kept an eye on what Caramello filched from the police. You wouldn't have got as far as you have in putting the puzzle together if it hadn't been for old Winkle!"

Packy clapped the old man on the back. "Thanks to you, Winkle, I'm beginning to remember a bit more. This is an exploding jigsaw puzzle. The information on it is too important to go unprotected in a wicked world. I recollect now, as soon as Silkweed, Fafner, and Mrs. Mangle attacked me in this very room, I pressed the detonating button and caused my jigsaw to self-destruct. That's what blew the wall out of this room, of course. At that very exact moment Silkweed struck me a blow that laid me out totally unconscious and caused me to lose my memory."

"Oh, the infamy!" cried Mrs. McTodd, and Jim clenched his fists to think that his brother had been treated so.

They crowded around Packy, urging him to try to remember more.

"I think it's all coming back," he said.

"And so am I!" said a hateful and well-remembered voice, and there in the doorway stood Dr. Silkweed, looking as

156

bored and languid as ever, carrying what looked like an old set of bagpipes. And just behind him came Mrs. Mangle, smiling a horrible, triumphant smile that showed every blue tooth in her head.

The captain whipped out his favorite sword in a second, and Mrs. Hatchett seized her saber, but Dr. Silkweed smiled odiously as if at a pair of impulsive infants.

"I really wouldn't," he said, "for should you make a threatening move I will instantly incinerate the children." Then they saw that what had seemed like bagpipes was actually the very flamethrower that had hung on the wall of his office in the academy. The friends of Humbert Cash-Cash were being threatened by his own invention. Silkweed had this fearsome weapon directly aimed at Annie, Wolfgang, and Caramello.

32　The Last of Mrs. Mangle

"So here we all are," said Dr. Silkweed. "How cozy. All's well that ends well, isn't it, Mrs. Hatchett? You would agree with William Shakespeare of course?"

"Indeed I do," said Mrs. Hatchett, adding grimly, "but Shakespeare also said, 'O that a man might know the end of this day's business ere it come!' "

"Now don't try to confuse me, I beg you," said Silkweed, yawning. "This is indeed the end. I'll be sorry to lose a promising bunch of Stubborn Orphans, but—" He gracefully helped himself to a cream puff from the refreshments on the table. "There are always more Stubborn Orphans. They're never really in short supply. The world, to its shame and my gratification, tosses them up as the sea tosses its shells and other rubbish onto the shore. I shall get some more. And who knows! There may even be another Humbert Cash-Cash among them. You aren't the first inventor, Humbert, and you won't be the last. A touch of this flamethrower (child of your own fertile imagination) and all your inventions will be mine to use for my own pleasure and profit."

"Hyperion! Hyperion!" cried Professor Fafner. "They actually putting together the jigsaw puzzle have been, and it is having on it the music to play on the school piano. You are being Emperor of Lightning at last."

"Excellent!" said Dr. Silkweed in a patronizing voice, but leaving Fafner tied firmly to the pillar.

Mrs. Mangle, surveying the faces glaring at her, noticed her onetime employers. "All the McTodds are here!" she exclaimed. "How nice to think they are all united as a family once more and will all go together when the moment comes."

Silkweed looked at Packy. "I didn't think of that damned jigsaw, you know. I thought it a mere trifle of childhood, not a collection of codes. But in your way you've always been a child, Humbert, with all the world nothing but a playground. Clever, though. Thank you all for piecing it together for me." He took a piece of Toad's pirate gingerbread. "Delicious! I do love a good bake of gingerbread."

"Hyperion!" Fafner let out a wail. "I wish to be untied."

"Alas, my dear Fafner!" Silkweed sighed. "You fail to understand your position. Ours has been a fruitful friendship, I won't deny, but I'm sure you'll be the first to appreciate that a man such as myself can hardly afford to tolerate failure. And here you are, left in a position of great responsibility and winding up prisoner of illiterate pirates and mere children. No, no—it's not good enough." He turned away from Fafner, pushing dusty little Caramello over without noticing. "You shall share the fate of our other guests and—er—go up in smoke." As he spoke he threw a sample burst of flame at the opening in the wall where the net instantly sizzled and vanished.

"Ah Humbert, Humbert," said Mrs. Mangle, "why did you desert us? Why did you run away and become rich and famous all on your own? How ungrateful to your guardians!"

"You were almost like a son to me," Dr. Silkweed said,

"and of course I couldn't help feeling that your inventions were really mine."

The pirates, orphans, and even Fafner said nothing. They looked as if they were staring at Silkweed and his sister, quite devoid of words, but they were really watching Caramello who had picked herself up and was standing at a corner of the table. The villains had their backs to her and could not see what everyone else could see, that she was holding the basket of Cash-Cash gingerbread. She quietly whisked away the plate of pirate gingerbread and replaced it with the Cash-Cash variety. So small and mouselike were her movements that neither Mrs. Mangle nor Dr. Silkweed noticed her at work right under their elbows.

"What? Dumbstruck?" asked Dr. Silkweed mockingly. "Nothing to say? Dear me. I thought you would be most eloquent. Who knows—if you beg for mercy I might consider sparing the children. No? I'm disappointed. Oh well . . ." He lifted the flamethrower.

"Avast there!" cried the pirate captain. "We're on a lee shore, I won't attempt to deny. Just give me a moment to think things over—just as long as it takes to eat a piece of gingerbread. I might beg for mercy a little bit then."

Dr. Silkweed was torn two ways. He longed to use the

160

flamethrower of course, and yet he longed to hear the pirate captain beg for mercy. He hesitated, shrugged, passed Mrs. Mangle a piece of gingerbread with rare brotherly consideration, and took a piece himself.

"Delicious!" he said, taking a large mouthful just as Mrs. Mangle did likewise. Pirates, orphans, Mrs. Hatchett, Thomas Sump, and the McTodds stood like people turned to stone. There was silence for a full second.

Then Dr. Silkweed and Mrs. Mangle both started to choke and scream, trying hard to do both at once. Silkweed dropped the flamethrower and clasped his hands to his throat, which suddenly seemed to him to be erupting with molten lava. He did a complete backward somersault in his alarm, dancing madly, gurgling, and turning such a bright red that ships far out at sea observed the glow through the hole in the wall. Mrs. Mangle turned a deep purple. The effect of uncontrolled Cash-Cash gingerbread was fearsome. The mighty heat generated by this mixture could have warmed frozen explorers back to life, but as it was, it seared the wicked siblings as if they had accidently swallowed burning coals. Tears poured from their eyes and their blackened tongues hung out like the tongues of terrible old shoes. Brace-and-Bit scooped up the flamethrower from the floor.

Mrs. Hatchett and the pirate captain both drew their swords. Thomas Sump picked up a chair, preparing for war, while the orphans leapt on Silkweed and Mangle, who struggled around in circles attempting to fight off the effects of the Cash-Cash gingerbread and the Stubborn Orphans at the same time.

It was obvious that Mrs. Mangle was trying to chant a spell, but the gingerbread had unstrung her vocal chords and she could only grimace and point. Not a word could she utter. Then her popping eyes fell on a great shadow

displayed on the back wall and somehow, in spite of everything, she did manage a faint wailing sound. Coming in
through the hole in the wall and landing with his wings
spread out and his claws forward, just like a duck landing
on a lagoon, was the great firedrake, Mangle. He landed
with a flapping and a scrabbling of claws.

"Evening all!" he cried cheerfully. "Where is it? I know
it's here! You can't fool me. I could smell it, you know,
and of course I just followed my nose as it were and ...
goodness gracious, what on earth is going on here? Is it a
party? Everyone standing around watching two dance vio-
lently with a gang of disreputable children."

Mrs. Mangle could not speak. She began to wave her

arms in the firedrake's direction, trying to cast a spell, but this was a mistake as it only attracted his attention. It was true he turned a bright green, but that wasn't much. It wouldn't worry an average firedrake for a second. In fact he seemed pleased rather than annoyed and studied her more closely.

"It is—it really is . . ." he murmured, "it's my wife, Ivy Mangle. After all these years! And who is that other one you're sitting on, children?"

"It's her brother, Dr. Silkweed!" cried Annie. "He ate some Cash-Cash gingerbread, and we've grabbed his flamethrower from him. Now we're going to keep him prisoner too. They're crooks and we've caught them."

"I am helping to tie him up," piped Fafner. "For why? My enemy, now, he is."

"I suppose that leaves me to look after my wife," said the firedrake. "Don't let her arms go. Because first I must have some of that gingerbread. I've never forgotten it. There I was, back on Island Eight Eight Eight and I smelled it baking. Well, I just had to come out of my hole and find out where that fascinating aroma was coming from. I've been working my way in and out of the Thousand Islands for hours."

Caramello offered him all the Cash-Cash gingerbread that was left and he ate it in a single mouthful.

"Lovely," he said, licking his lips with a tongue like a welding torch. "Lovely! Just right for a firedrake. Any more? Well, never mind! All good things must come to an end. Now let me see—Ivy—hmm! I think I can remember that spell, though when you've only heard it once it sometimes is a little difficult. Still . . ." He closed his eyes and began mumbling. Mrs. Mangle tried to scream but only managed the merest squeak. Before their eyes, between the mighty hands of Thomas Sump who was holding her prisoner, she began to change until even Sump was forced to let her go. Her nose grew into a long snout, silver scales covered her body, her slippers, her flowery apron and even the Warlock's Whizzbang for Advanced Wickedness all fell from her. She had become a firedrake, smaller than her husband but extremely formidable. And, with her new throat, she was able to talk quite clearly.

"Well really, Mangle, darling!" she exclaimed. "I didn't know you cared. And after the way I treated you too."

"It's not bad being a firedrake," Mangle cried eagerly. "But—I don't know—the fact is I've missed you, Ivy. It's true you've got some funny ways, being treacherous and so on, but we firedrakes like that in a wife. It's the challenge, you see! Now, there's a spare hole on Island Eight Eight Eight, quite close to mine, where you could live very com-

fortably. Oh, there's a pile of treasure in it but don't let that bother you. Just throw out the bits you don't fancy."

The funny thing is that Mrs. Mangle looked a lot better as a firedrake than she had as a witch. She glittered all over as if sewn with sequins, and she had a beautiful long tail which she could swish around. She looked slender and elegant, like some lovely Christmas decoration, and she seemed to realize this with pleasure.

"Oh Mangle!" she cried. "All this time, deep down, you've loved me. What faithfulness! And I have never ceased to adore you. Remember I sent you those explorers, and insurance salesmen. You have been ever present in my heart. Is there any more of that delightful gingerbread left?"

Toad coughed modestly and said it was all gone.

"I'll bring you some more, however," he promised, "as soon as we all settle down and find out what's what."

"By the powers!" exclaimed Brace-and-Bit. "He'll bake a batch and we'll bring it to you on Island Eight Eight Eight ... Cash-Cash gingerbread, the gingerbread of Eskimos and firedrakes."

"Oh well, if there's no more we'll be off, then," declared Mangle. "Come on, Ivy! Forget about that brother of yours. He's needed someone to sit on him for years, and I'm glad these fine pirates have done it. Your only fault was having Silkweed for a brother, and now that he's taken care of, you seem quite perfect."

"Funny!" said Mrs. Mangle. "Now that I'm a firedrake I find I don't care for him very much myself. He was so stuck up about having a mere flamethrower too. All right, Mangle, let's be off!"

And she flew away through the hole in the wall with a great flapping of her new wings.

Mangle hesitated and looked at the pirates.

165

"I'll keep her out of your way from now on," he said. "You may think it's weak of me to forgive her, but I adore that bewitching creature. Now don't forget the gingerbread, will you? Terrible if we had to come looking for it." And with a wave of one claw he soared off to give praise and assistance to Mrs. Mangle, who was having trouble keeping aloft.

"Flap from the shoulder, Ivy," they heard him shouting. "You're flapping from the elbow. You're losing all your power. Take the time from me. *One,* two, three, four! Off we go, my darling!"

"Never a dull moment!" said Mrs. Hatchett, feeling the edge of her saber and smiling.

33 THE GOLDEN BALLOON

No sooner had Mrs. Hatchett spoken these words than a posse of policemen erupted into the room, followed by Detective Inspector Carstairs who took in the situation at a glance. A sudden silence fell.

"I call for the assistance of the law," cried Silkweed faintly, for he was lying on the floor with all the McTodds standing on him in a row.

"Let me explain ..." began the captain, in a trembling voice. "There's a reason for all this."

Detective Inspector Carstairs gave him a wonderful smile. She was holding a thick pile of pages, all held together by a Hookywalker Police Department clip.

"You need say no more," she told him, "or not much more anyway. This account was found by our patrolling police launch floating in the Hookywalker harbor. It has told us almost all we need to know."

"Look!" shouted Annie. "It's that story you got me to write down ... all about Mrs. Mangle and the firedrake and finding Packy in the packing case and ..."

"And my confession about stealing the piano!" rumbled Thomas Sump. "And the tale of Silkweed's wicked ways, and his false accusations, and so on. I thought it had all been lost in the Everlasting Whirlwind."

"I have studied it from beginning to end," said Carstairs, "and it has cleared up many mysteries. Ah, this must be

James McTodd. I am glad to see you well after your terrible ordeal. And this—this must be Humbert Cash-Cash."

She really doesn't know him, thought the captain with relief.

Meanwhile her task force, led by Bogtrotter and Robertson, handcuffed Silkweed. Tied with Fafner's own shoelaces, and marked with the footprints of the McTodd family, he was dragged off toward the library door. As he went he gave a maniacal cackle.

"Cash-Cash will never now have the power to direct lightning. His greatest invention is mine! The vital code is not in his memory, nor in the jigsaw puzzle, it is in the piano, and that is hidden where you will never find it."

"You couldn't have moved the piano without me!" cried Thomas Sump, shocked to the depths of his piano-mover's soul.

"Of course he couldn't," said the captain. "He's bluffing."

"Am I? Ha, ha, ha!" Even defeated, Silkweed sounded sinister.

Caramello gave a chuckle too. She was an odd child, no doubt about it.

Suddenly the view through the missing wall was filled with a wonderful sight: The beautiful balloon they had often seen in the sky hovered above them. An anchor was cast out, firmly attaching the balloon to the island, and then a ladder of silver rope came snaking down into the garden. Immediately baboons and wolves clustered around, staring upward expectantly.

Everyone rushed out into the garden, anxious to prevent them from tearing the balloonist to pieces, but they had no need to worry.

It was a lovely young woman with eyes the color of melting chocolate and a chin as pretty as that of Detective

168

Inspector Carstairs. However, instead of golden curls the balloonist had long, slinky, chestnut locks. They didn't look quite like sisters but they could almost have been cousins.

"Caterina!" cried Packy.

"Packy!" cried Caterina.

"Mummy!" cried Caramello.

"My little Nell!" And Caterina scooped up her small daughter in her arms and kissed her husband, to whom everything had suddenly become crystal clear.

Everyone started talking at once, jumping with excitement, including the wolves and baboons, the only ones to have been worried about their missing mistress.

"Mother, Father," said Packy, "this is my wife, Caterina. Caterina, I've found my missing parents."

"A daughter-in-law! What a surprise!" said Mrs. McTodd, greeting her warmly.

"A mother-in-law! How lovely!" cried Caterina, greeting her in return.

"And a granddaughter," exclaimed Mrs. McTodd, "named after me!"

It came as a shock to the pirates to realize that Caramello's name was really Nell after all, but by then everyone was so used to calling her by her orphanage name they decided not to change it right away.

"It might be confusing, her having two names," said Winkle doubtfully.

"After what we've been through we'll cope with two names easily enough," cried Captain Wafer with feeling. "Two names will be sheer simplicity to us."

When all the embracing was over, Packy said, gazing fondly at his wife, "I'd have been home before, my dear, but I lost my memory."

"How like you, darling!" she exclaimed. "He's always losing something," she told the assembled company. "He loses his pencils, his way, and sometimes even his temper, if I'm not at hand to stop him. And of course I'm often out, breaking records in my hot-air balloon. I fly under my maiden name," she added modestly.

"Are you my cousin, Caterina Wolfspangle, the well-known hot-air balloonist?" cried Detective Inspector Carstairs, and Caterina dimpled prettily as she admitted she was.

"Oh, joy! Another celebrity in the family," cried the

McTodds, embracing her (and then one another) yet again.

"I was just coming home after a vigorous afternoon bal-
looning when Silkweed struck," said Caterina. "I couldn't
believe my eyes when I saw our home explode. The force
of the explosion tossed my balloon around quite a lot, but
thanks to Packy's steering device for hot-air balloons, I had
no difficulty in controlling it. When I saw them carrying
the blue packing case down to the boat I was sure that
Silkweed had kidnapped my dear husband, so I followed,
sustaining myself from time to time with a little cham-
pagne, and Packy's feast cubes. I have a minifridge in the
hot-air balloon that is full of them. They're delicious.

"Of course I saw through my telescope that the packing
case was actually full of encyclopedias, and immediately I
realized that Packy was probably in the *other* case, which
had gone bobbing off over the sea. It was a terrible moment, for I had to leave my little daughter at the Deadlock
Orphanage. But at least I knew where you were, darling,"
said Caterina in a loving voice to Caramello. "And there
was poor Daddy bouncing up and down among the Thousand Islands. I knew you were quite capable of coping with
the Deadlock Orphanage, just like your father before you."

"That's all right, Mommy," cried Caramello. "I pretended I couldn't speak, and that saved me from having to answer a lot of silly questions. I saw your balloon over Thomas Sump's shoulder as he carried me along, and I hoped you'd go after Daddy. His need was greater than mine."

"What a little angel," cried the McTodds adoringly. But Silkweed gave her a bitter glance.

"I am perfectly sure the piano has been taken by helicopter to the Deadlock Orphanage," Caramello said. "The matron, Mrs. Tiberius, has a room with a trapdoor in the roof. I found out a lot of things about the place during my stay there. I found Towelly, for example."

"What talent!" cried the McTodds, but Silkweed bayed with fury, like a timber wolf. He fell back, foaming with rage, into the arms of Bogtrotter and Robertson, who were having a difficult, though exciting, time controlling not only Silkweed but Fafner, who was lashing around in pretended remorse. All in vain! Fafner and Silkweed were chained together and taken down to the jetty.

"I watched you rescue my husband," Caterina cried to Captain Wafer. "What happiness was mine when I saw him rising out of the pink-and-white tissue paper like Venus from the foam. I was about to land on the deck and claim him when I thought that it might be a good idea to come home and see what was going on here. There was no sense in bringing him back only to have him taken away from me because of some vile trap of Silkweed's. And after that, things got a little out of hand. I lost track of you entirely. How could I guess that Packy had lost his memory, and that you had all set off to learn reading at the Silkweed Academy?"

Everyone agreed that this would have been hard to guess even on solid ground, let alone up in a balloon.

"When I found *The Sinful Sausage* it was deserted, moored at the smuggler's cove, and shortly after that I was caught up in the Everlasting Whirlwind. I was quite all right, of course, but it did take me a while to get out of it, and then it was only to see you on Dessert Island. Shortly after that you set off on your way here. I could smell the familiar smell of Cash-Cash gingerbread. And I saw a firedrake following you. But here you are at last and here I am, and here we all are."

34 Back to Real Life

There was an air of joy and romance on Island Six Hundred and Sixty-six that penetrated even the most redoubtable hearts.

"Thomas!" said Mrs. Hatchett. "I don't entirely blame you for stealing that piano. But it shows you are not safe to be let out alone if you fall among thieves at the drop of a hat. I shall marry you and keep you in order from now on."

"Oh glory, glory!" cried Thomas Sump, an expression of exaltation on his battered face, and he embraced her, regardless of her spiked belt.

Now that the adventure seemed to be over there was something a little wistful about the way the orphans looked out across the sea. Carstairs watched the police launch heading back to Hookywalker with its criminal cargo. And down by the jetty was the good old *Sinful Sausage* riding placidly at anchor, the Jolly Roger and Towelly both at the masthead, Towelly fluttering cheerfully in a breeze that had not quite arrived but was probably on its way.

Captain Wafer was just about to take Carstairs by the hand when she suddenly exclaimed in a puzzled voice, "Look at that. One of your flags is streaming out in the wind and the other isn't. How curious."

"That's not a flag," Annie said. "It's Towelly, and it's often a little bit ahead of the rest of us in time."

"What!" cried Carstairs, snatching a small, folding telescope from Caterina's belt. "I've only heard of one object that was ahead of the rest of the world in time. It was stitched in a very pious convent where the clocks were two-and-a-half minutes fast and—now, let me see . . ."

She studied Towelly through her telescope. Her hands began to tremble with excitement and she was unable to hold the telescope still.

"To whom does Towelly belong?" she asked at last.

"Well, to Caramello mostly!" Wolfgang said. "She found it in the bathroom cupboard at the Deadlock Orphanage."

"I couldn't be mistaken," Carstairs said in a solemn voice. "I have studied the list of missing art treasures of our land too often to make a mistake. That is the Noah's Ark Tapestry* of the Hookywalker Museum, and though it is very grubby I'm sure it will be all right when it is cleaned in the proper way. There is a big reward offered for it. Two hundred thousand dollars, or pounds or something. You will be the richest orphans in the world."

---

*Just how this rare art treasure came to be in the bathroom cupboard of the Deadlock Orphanage is a long tale, so complicated that this story you've just read is a miracle of simplicity compared with it. And it is too close to the end of the book to go into it now.

"Two hundred thousand of something!" cried Wolfgang, his face lighting up.

"Do you realize what that means?" asked Annie, from under her bangs.

"Yes of course!" shouted Wolfgang. "I was thinking our adventures were over but this is the best thing yet. *I* think so, anyway."

Annie got down to business at once.

"Mr. and Mrs. McTodd, we'd like to buy Dessert Island," she said. "We're going to be able to give you a hundred thousand of something and have a bit over for ourselves. We'll maintain the island just as you would wish, making puddings and cakes and so on in the Mc-Todd tradition. Do sell it to us as soon as you can."

"We will!" old McTodd said. "For we are going to live here from now on with our two sons, our daughter-in-law, and our little granddaughter. Come inside once more, and we will work out details of the transfer of Dessert Island, the Christmas–cake house, and assorted recipes. Oh, what a happy day this is for all!"

Lives were being arranged, fortunes were dropping into place, for everyone except the pirates, whose future was still uncertain. It was true they had solved their mysteries but they were still as poor as ever and couldn't help feeling, moreover, that the simple life they had sought had turned out too complicated for any reasonable man to tolerate. But pirates are men of action.

The captain straightened his shoulders and smoothed his gallant beard. "Detective Inspector Carstairs," he exclaimed, "I am not one of your introspective, secretive pirates but a straightforward sea dog and I declare, before witnesses, that I love you from the bottom of my boots."

"He's been but a shadow of his former self," Toad put in. "You have conquered that proud heart."

"Rumblebumpkin! Silence!" swore the captain. "Let me do my own proposing." To Carstairs he said, "I am offering you the deepest devotion a dashing sea dog ever offered a detective inspector."

"Well, I accept," said Carstairs with beautiful simplicity. "I have loved you with a mad passion from the time I first saw you sitting sulkily in Silkweed's Academy."

"Oh, Captain!" wavered Winkle. "She loves you. Isn't that nice!"

"You love me?" the captain could hardly believe his ears, and Toad was actually seen to shake his out in sheer disbelief. "But how can it be? I am a pirate, a proud, unprincipled profligate, peppered with imperfections—possibly penitent but probably past praying for, and you are a detective inspector devoted to duty and decency, deferring to dignity and degree. How can we dare to hope for happiness together?"

"Well, I'll tell you!" Carstairs said. "I've been working something out. I have had tremendous triumphs solving mysteries and bringing malefactors to justice, so that I have become renowned and recognized everywhere. It is no longer possible to do undercover work. My fame goes before me among all my suspects. Secret investigations are ruined. I plan to leave the Hookywalker Detective Department and take up a totally different profession."

"What do you have in mind?" asked the pirate captain keenly.

"Well, call me romantic if you will," said Detective Inspector Carstairs, smiling, "but I have dreamed of starting a little tearoom on the Hookywalker waterfront. There are lots of tourists to be found there walking up and down and longing for refreshment. A rather dashing tearoom I think—with rum babas and brandysnaps, and so on. If you agree, we could give it a nautical flavor—just as a tribute to your own profession. Our waiters could dress as pirates, for example."

Detective Inspector Carstairs and the pirate captain kissed each other, while Brace-and-Bit and Toad beamed at them

like fairy godfathers, and Winkle gaped with amazement.

"Then," went on Carstairs, "when people see me wearing a spotted neckerchief and a rather becoming eye patch while serving ice cream, they will soon forget I was a famous detective, and after a little while I could resume my former secret activities with you and your mates to help me. No one would suspect for a moment that their sins were under observation from an innocent tearoom."

"Better and better," cried the captain. "No more of the single life! It's the double life for me!"

"It was supposed to be the simple life we were after," Winkle said. "Not that it has been simple!" he added hastily.

"Doom again!" squawked Toothpick, as self-satisfied as ever.

Out rushed the Stubborn Orphans from their business conference, and out came the old McTodds.

"We've done it," Annie shouted. "We've bought Dessert Island. All we have to do is to get the reward for Towelly, and Dessert Island is ours."

"And unlimited pudding," added Wolfgang. "I couldn't be happier!"

"Look!" said old McTodd. He pointed toward the glowing western sky. "Ivy Silkweed! Just imagine!"

Far away, over what was almost certainly Island Eight Hundred and Eighty-eight, two firedrakes swirled up into the air, making elegant loops of flame as they flew. Higher and higher they spun, fighting or dancing (Who could tell?) but obviously enjoying themselves either way.

"Well, as far as I can see we might as well have stayed in real life in the first place," said Winkle, shaking his white head, "because the simple life is very difficult to come by. You see it far off, like Island One Thousand as it might be, but by the time you catch up with it, it's got all mixed up with a whole lot of other stuff."

He was right of course, but nobody paid any attention to Winkle.

Margaret Mahy

is the author of several acclaimed Dial books, including *The Boy Who Was Followed Home,* an ALA Notable, illustrated by Steven Kellogg; *17 Kings and 42 Elephants,* a *New York Times* Best Illustrated Book, with pictures by Patricia MacCarthy; and *The Great White Man-Eating Shark,* a *School Library Journal* Best Book of the Year, illustrated by Jonathan Allen. Among her novels for young readers are *The Haunting* and the ALA Notable *Changeover: A Supernatural Romance,* both of which won the prestigious Carnegie Medal in Great Britain. Ms. Mahy was a children's librarian before turning to writing full-time. She has two daughters and lives in New Zealand.

Margaret Chamberlain

has illustrated many children's books, including *The Man Whose Mother Was a Pirate* (Puffin) and other titles by Ms. Mahy. She lives near Bath, England.